Mira's Last DANCE

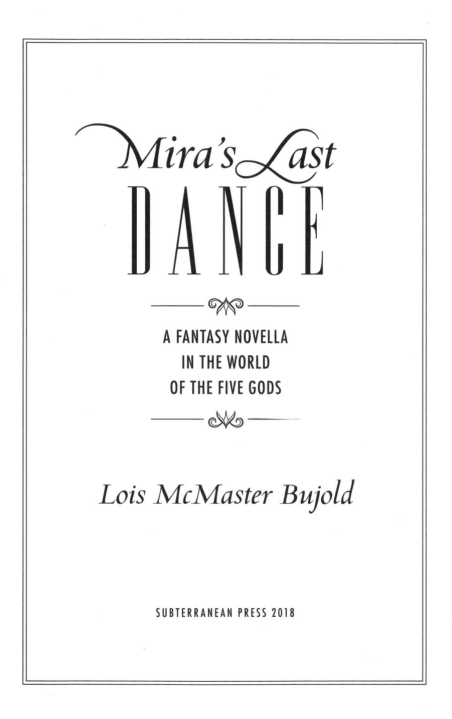

Mira's Last
DANCE

A FANTASY NOVELLA
IN THE WORLD
OF THE FIVE GODS

Lois McMaster Bujold

SUBTERRANEAN PRESS 2018

First Hardcover Edition

ISBN
978-1-59606-854-4

Subterranean Press
PO Box 190106
Burton, MI 48519

subterraneanpress.com

I

NIKYS WAS WORRIED about their sorcerer. They'd fetched up at this little hill-country farmhouse two days ago, passing off their disheveled party of three as a man and his wife, plus their friend who'd sprained his ankle when they'd lost their way on the rocky trails in the dark. Their coin spoke more convincingly than they did, she'd suspected. What seemed to her a small sum had bought them shelter, displacing the farmer couple from their whitewashed bedroom to the loft and their half-grown children in turn to the stable. Such rural hospitality would cost their hosts a great deal more trouble than that if Imperial pursuers arrived here, Nikys reflected uneasily. She rocked her hips to bump open the bedroom door, and carried her tray within.

Learned Penric was dutifully lying flat in the bed, as ordered, but not asleep. He hitched himself up on one elbow, blinking glazed blue eyes at her, and favored her with one of his strange sweet smiles. Quite as if he hadn't *almost died* three nights ago, defending her and her brother Adelis.

"Ah. Another meal, already?"

"I'm sure you need it. Or Desdemona does." Penric might just be one of those maddening long, lean people who could eat like a horse and never gain a bit of pudge, but she guessed his chaos demon, riding inside him like a second personality—a very complicated second personality—drew on his body for nourishment as well. "Do you have to eat for two?"

"Mm, maybe a little. Here, I can get up—"

"Lie back!" Nikys and Desdemona commanded together. Since Des spoke through Penric's mouth, the effect was quite peculiar, but Nikys fancied she was getting used to it. "Listen to your demonic physician," Nikys said, to which Des added, "Yes, and listen to your lovely nurse. She knows what she's about in the sickroom."

"When did you two combine forces?" Penric muttered, as Nikys set down the tray on the wash-stand and drew it to the bedside, plumped his pillows, and permitted him to sit up. "Here, you don't need to spoon-feed me."

"It's not soup, so I can't." Nikys plopped down beside him, spread goat cheese onto circles of coarse country flatbread, added sliced onion, and rolled them up, alternating handing them across with holding the beaker of watered wine. Penric tried to take the vessel one-handed, but ended up having to use two, as his hand shook. He cast her an evasive look through those unreasonably long blond eyelashes.

Not for the first time, Nikys wondered exactly what it *meant* that the rival sorcerer, whom Pen had defeated in that bizarre twilight fight, had tried to rip his heart apart inside his body, and how much magical work Desdemona had been doing every moment since to keep it beating. Her own and Adelis's father, old General Arisaydia, had survived half-a-dozen bloody military campaigns in his life, only to die of a sudden seizure of the heart. That final, fatal blow had made no mark upon him. Bad hearts frightened her.

Nikys finished coaxing the whole of her culinary offering down the not-unwilling man. The fact that Penric was out of breath from eating lunch was more telling than his panting protestations of recovery. She checked the artistic bandage around his right ankle, mainly placed there to help him remember which one was supposed to be sprained, and tightened it up again.

The discreet blond knot at his nape had unraveled into a tangled mess. "I have a comb," Nikys went on, drawing it from the pocket of her borrowed apron. "I can straighten out those snarls of yours." She'd wanted an excuse to touch that amazing electrum hair for weeks, ever since he'd appeared like an improbable guardian spirit in her villa garden, offering healing for her unjustly blinded brother.

He started to indignantly refuse, and then either his wits or his demon caught up with him. He swallowed his manly declaration of self-sufficiency, converting it into a hopeful smile. "That would be very nice."

She had him sit up on the edge of the bed and knelt behind him. The rope net strung on the bedframe, topped by the wool-stuffed mattress, was not the firmest of seating, and his narrow hips rather sank between her knees. She began at the bottom of the tail of hair that reached to his mid-back, working out the knots as though carding fine flax. He'd kept himself as clean as a cat back in the villa in Patos, as became a physician, but they were all the worse for wear after a week's flight. She wondered if she could persuade him to let her wash it for him. She just might, judging by the way he was making low humming noises, as close to a purr as a human could come, as the tortoiseshell tines reached his neck and scalp and began slow, repeated strokes.

Alternating the comb and her gratified fingers, she began to separate the soft length into three strands for braiding, only to discover that somehow there was no room left for the task between his bony back and her...un-bony front. She cleared her throat and inched back, and he seemed to come awake and lurched forward, bowed spine straightening, once again the tidy Temple divine. Albeit a divine sworn to the Bastard, the fifth god, whose emblematic color was a white in real life usually ambiguously stained. She'd sometimes wondered if that was the white god's idea of theological humor. Laundresses should be in His flock, really; they probably served Him on their knees more often than did divines.

Learned Penric cleared his throat, too, and she caught a glimpse past his ear of milk-pale cheekbone faintly flushed.

She set to finishing the queue and tying it off—she'd snipped the bit of white ribbon from one of her few garments that she'd managed to grab when they'd escaped the soldiers in Patos. An undefeated enemy, still out there on the hunt. The memory was enough to chill her brief warm comfort. Just as well; she had barely time to slide off the bed and tuck Penric back into it as the distinctive clunk of her brother's boots sounded across the farmhouse floorboards and through the door.

"There you are."

Adelis looked, really, almost his old self, at least from the mouth down. Standing straight again, sturdy, muscular; his thirty years sat lightly upon young General Arisaydia. Young former-general Arisaydia. Only when he took off his countryman's broad-brimmed hat did the horror of the burn-scarring on his upper face spring out. A barely healed spray of red and raised pink welts bloomed like malign flower petals around his eyes, though Penric claimed they would someday fade pale. His formerly dark brown irises had been resurrected a garnet red from their acid destruction. But thanks to Penric's sorcerous healing he could see again, and well, apparently, which in Nikys's view went somewhere beyond magic to miracle.

Adelis ran a hand through his black hair, growing unmilitarily untrimmed, and addressed a point in the air between his sister and the man in the bed. "How is he doing?"

"All right," answered Penric.

"Not as well as he claims," Nikys corrected this. "Desdemona says he shouldn't do any lifting or sudden exertion, so as not to strain his healing heart."

"Hnh," said Adelis. He focused on Penric. "Do you think you could ride tomorrow? Led at a walk?"

"Not on that poor donkey in the yard. My feet would drag the ground," said Penric.

Adelis's shrug acknowledged the truth of this. "I've found a neighbor lad with a mule. He can't take us all the way to the Duchy of Orbas, but he can take us down to a cousin's farm in the valley. Which would at least put us farther from the pass that they know we hiked over. We're not safe here for long."

Penric nodded; Nikys frowned. Penric put in, "A change of scene wouldn't hurt. Des has pretty much eradicated all the small pests within range, shedding chaos. We could do with a new supply."

His demon traded out the disorder harvested from his sorcerous healings, as Nikys understood it, venting it into the world as safely as they could manage. Killing theologically allowed vermin, the divine claimed, was the most efficient such sink available. Other sinks were less efficient. Or less allowed. She contemplated the dangerous gap between *not allowed* and *not possible*. Did Penric know where the real boundaries lay? She hoped so.

"We'll go at dawn, then," said Adelis.

IN THE event, it was full light when they finally loaded Penric, still short-winded, and their few possessions aboard the tall and placid mule. Adelis's stolen sword and bow and arrows traveled wrapped in cloth, a discretion that didn't content him much. Nikys was just as glad. She didn't doubt her brother would fight to the death before allowing himself to be captured again, but it seemed pointless to send stranger-souls unripe to their gods if it made no difference to the outcome. Penric's glib tongue might be a better defense than Adelis's sword arm. Or indeed, Penric's magic, though his demon was very quiet this morning. Busy within him still healing his hidden damage, she guessed from the occasional flies, buzzing up from animal droppings on the farm track, that fell dead in their wake. She trusted the mule-boy didn't notice.

The presence of this youth leading the mule inhibited conversation on the long trudge, thankfully more downhill than not. The farm track, which eventually grew to a farm road, followed a winding creek with the hills rising on either side. Nikys was hot, sweaty, and footsore by the noon halt, where the boy led them out onto a local promontory shaded by old oaks, evidently a favorite stop. She could see why. It offered a last high view out over the miles-wide valley that made this province such a valuable, and defended, granary for the Cedonian empire.

The mule-boy led his charge off to a distant patch of grass for its own lunch. Adelis strolled to the rim above the drop-off, pushed back his hat, and stared with eyes narrowed. Nikys and Penric joined him.

"This is as good as a map," Penric remarked, following his gaze. "What are we looking at?"

Adelis dipped his chin. "The walled town on that bit of height above the river is Sosie. Not the capital of the province, that's down by the mouth with the port. But it's home to the garrison that guards the top end of this valley." His hand sketched out the squared-off patch, vague in the distance, that suggested barracks. "Imperial troops, not provincial. Part of the Fourteenth Infantry."

"That sounds like something we might need to avoid," said Penric. "Would any of them recognize you?"

Adelis's hand touched his still-tender face. "I wonder."

"The three of us are distinctive, if any description has been circulated yet," Nikys observed unhappily. Even if not together, Adelis's disfigurement and Penric's height and foreign coloration would make them stand out. Only Nikys might pass unremarked.

"Still, Sosie has a large temple," said Adelis. Its stone shape was just visible, rising on a hill within the city walls. "Might you, ah, refresh your purse there?" He cast Penric a sidewise look.

Penric's expression was more grimace than smile. "I should not like to make a settled habit of robbing offering boxes. Although it's still better than robbing people directly. It's money they've already given up, and so presumably will not miss." He mused on, whether talking himself into or out of the suggestion Nikys could not tell, "Hard on the local temple, though. You would not believe Temple expenses."

"But we could hire horses again, or even some sort of carriage," Nikys couldn't help noting. Her tired feet talking, to be sure, but a carriage might be better for the convalescent sorcerer as well.

"By what route?" asked Penric.

"Only two choices," said Adelis. "Well, three. We could make our way down the valley to the coast road, or even to a port for some local ship to take us south."

"That was my suggestion in the last valley," Penric noted a bit dryly. "We could have saved steps."

Adelis stiffly ignored this, and continued, "Either will be well guarded. And I guarantee any description of us will be sent to the border posts and ports first. The other way would be to find a path up through the mountains to Orbas."

The rocky walls lining the other side of the valley were considerably more daunting than the hills they had just come over. Which was a good part of why the current duke of Orbas was able to maintain his precarious independence from a neighbor who would be very pleased to turn his lands back into an imperial province. Nikys had always felt that Cedonia had the right of that old dispute, before.

Penric stared at the distant precipices, too, and finally said, "Unless we could pass in disguise."

"I am not putting on Nikys's clothes again," said Adelis, scowling.

Penric grinned, provokingly. "True, you did not make a very convincing widow."

"I'm an officer. Not an actor." A brief clench of his jaw suggested to Nikys that he was remembering he was neither, now.

"In any case," said Nikys, placating, "our roads lie together till we reach Vilnoc in Orbas. Penric can as well sail home to Adria from there." *Or not...*

"Or we all could," Penric suggested. Yet again.

"Nikys and I are going to Orbas," said Adelis. "You may go where you please."

Penric studied his set face, and sighed.

And if neither man—one as stubborn as a stone, the other too supple to be pinned down—would, or even could, change his mind, where would that leave Nikys? *No place happy.*

After eating, they resumed the downward trek. Penric, watching Nikys stump along, apparently forgot his sprained ankle and offered to trade her his place on the mule. For the mule-boy's benefit, Nikys asked after his fictional crippling, keeping his real one to herself, and he subsided, gallantry thwarted. But the mule-boy allowed as how they might ride double. Nikys was duly boosted onto the beast behind Penric, wriggling her way to comfort atop the blanket strapped to its barrel. Neither the mule nor Adelis seemed best pleased with this cozy new arrangement, but they didn't kick. Nikys slipped her arms around Penric's waist, for security, and he sat back a little, for what reason she did not speculate. Weary in the warm afternoon, she leaned her head against his shoulder and half dozed, the thousand worries coursing through her mind easing their torrent for a time.

ARRIVING AT the next farmstead in the early evening, they negotiated shelter with nearly the last of their coin. The combination of their thin purse and a house full of farm family left the stable loft the sole choice for their new bedroom. Adelis and Penric were both apologetic about it. Nikys was too tired to complain even if she had been a fussy fool, which she was not. This more fertile stretch of country also assured a good supply of stored grain, hence an abundance of the mice and rats that infested such. Desdemona was pleased. Penric, swinging a stick that he occasionally remembered to lean on, puffed off in the dark to hunt them for all the world like a cat.

Adelis hooked the lantern on a nail safely away from the straw, and rather pointedly arranged their blankets with himself in the middle as a bolster. Nikys snickered.

"I haven't been a girl laying flowers on the altar of the Daughter of Spring"—goddess of, among other things, virginity—"for over a decade," she pointed out.

"One wouldn't know it, from the infatuated way you were hanging on that sorcerer's shoulder all afternoon."

"You don't, actually, have a right to tell your thirty-year-old widowed sister who and who not to cuddle." Should it please her to cuddle anyone, which it hadn't for a very long, gray time.

Adelis lowered himself to their straw pile with a grunt, looking unhappy. On the whole, Nikys thought she'd rather deal with grouchy, where she could give as good, or as bad, as she got. "Think it through. I know what wonders the man has done for us, and I'm not ungrateful, but he's an Adriac agent, for the five gods' sake. Sent here to suborn me, till *that* plan went wrong in so many ways. He hasn't stopped being one, for all that I've chosen to go supplicant to Duke Jurgo of Orbas instead. Suppose, in the best case, we all win through to Vilnoc alive. The man will have no choice then but to go on home, empty-handed. Don't get...don't get taken in, is all I ask. You don't want to end up with nothing but a blue-eyed infant to remember him by."

Nikys was not altogether sure she'd object to such a souvenir, but she snorted. "I had six years of marriage with Kymis, which left me with less than that. And it wasn't for lack of trying, I assure you. I don't think it's a pressing danger." Although her late husband's frequent and prolonged absences on military duties hadn't helped. "Anyway, I doubt Learned Penric's up to seducing anyone, in his current condition."

Adelis was drawn into a sly smirk. "Quite. We wouldn't want the poor man dropping of an apoplexy between your thighs."

"Adelis!" Deterring image indeed.

"Truth, it's happened! I've heard. Although generally with older men."

She threw straw at him. He threw it back. Before they could revert further to their five-year-old selves, she heard the squeak of the stable door, the object of their argument returning. She bit back retaliating rudeness. But she did think to add, "You should want to keep him with you anyway, at least until you gain a position from Duke Jurgo. It will give you a much stronger position to negotiate from if Jurgo knows, or at least believes, that you have another offer waiting. Not supplicant, but, but…"

"Merchant?" he said dryly. "With myself as both seller and horse?"

"Think it through," she shot his own words back at him, and he raised a hand in concession.

THEY LAID up at the valley farm for two days. Adelis kept out of sight in the loft, growing bored and restless. Penric only descended to vent chaos when the farm folk were abed, though he evidently was able to vent quite a lot. On the bright side, he seemed to be recovering his strength and wind, but Desdemona's labors were creating a growing reek of dead rodent about the place.

Sitting up cross-legged on his blanket in the warmth of the afternoon, Penric sniffed apprehensively at a particularly pungent waft. "Huh. I don't normally leave such an obvious swathe in one place. People are going to notice, I'm afraid."

"I should think they'd be grateful," said Nikys. Although it would be better if people didn't learn he was a sorcerer, since their pursuers must by now be looking for one.

"You'd be surprised. Once, when I was a young student, I freed a man of his body lice without asking. He nearly had a fit. I hadn't realized he'd thought of them as pets. He was certain it indicated some terrible loss of health, like rats deserting a sinking ship. I wasn't in a place where I could explain my calling, so I ended up tiptoeing away."

"Why couldn't you explain what you'd done?" asked Nikys.

"We were in a gambling hall. I wasn't cheating, but proving it would have been a challenge."

Adelis snorted. "You'd have been beaten up, more likely."

Nikys tilted her head, trying to picture a young Penric so cornered. "Would you have let yourself be?"

He shrugged. "There was nothing at stake but an evening's entertainment. Heroic measures were not called for. Hence the tiptoeing. We should do likewise, soon."

It was left this time for Nikys to arrange it. Asking among the farm women turned up word of a neighbor taking a wain load of grain to Sosie, which they caught in the gray of the next dawn in exchange for their last coins and the promise of Adelis's shoulder should the wheels bog. It was a long day's ride at the oxen's steady pace, but they entered the city gates before dark. Passing their bedraggled selves off to the gate guards as rustic laborers was no trouble at all. They dropped down from the wagon near the temple and waved farewell to the grain man.

Penric had promised them a night of secret shelter in the temple atrium, once he'd slipped them all inside and relocked the doors. Nikys looked forward to the safety, if not to the discomfort. It seemed to her their bedding as well as their endurance was steadily deteriorating as this flight staggered on. And the refuge of Orbas, so close, still hovered maddeningly out of reach.

II

---

*I*N THE DWINDLING daylight, Penric threaded the
narrow streets of Sosie to the temple square.
Leading his flock of two, though Arisaydia and his
sister were anything but lamb-like. The space boasted
a small fountain, and some stone benches scattered
about, gifts of some pious rich benefactor according
to the inscriptions chiseled upon them in the elegant
lettering of Old Cedonian. Penric selected the most
shadowed bench and settled them all down to wait
for the square to clear as full night fell.

Nikys brought out the last of their bread from
the farm and shared it among them. Adelis eased up
his lowered hat brim, squinting around in a tactical
survey as he chewed.

"I doubt the city watch will let us linger here much after curfew," he observed. "If Sosie is like other garrison towns, they'll be in perpetual feud with young soldiers from the barracks, and so be more active than the usual sleepy companies."

"Then perhaps they'll be too busy elsewhere to bother us," Nikys suggested in a tone of bracing hope.

Penric considered the picture they presented, huddled here like skulking vagrants. Just the sort of vagabonds to be suspected of potential thievery in the night. Perfectly correctly, in their case. While being arrested would give them a free place to stay, its other costs were likely to be much too high.

A small throng of townsfolk was assembling under the portico sheltering the temple entry. They spilled down the steps as a pair of acolytes came out and swung the doors wide, hooking them open and lighting cressets high on the stone walls to either side. Soon after, what was obviously a funeral procession emerged from one of the side streets: a pair of liveried servants bearing lanterns up on poles, six grim-faced men carrying a bier with a shrouded figure, kin dressed in hasty mourning following in a gaggle. Instead of entering the temple atrium, they paused. A faint golden glow of a sacred fire not banked for the night, but fed to flames, wavered through to the square. In a few more minutes, another procession emerged from another street. Its shrouded bier was piled about with flower garlands. The two processions came together in a sort of wary truce, then, carefully, both biers were lined up and carried within exactly side-by-side.

A squad of city watchmen followed. Half of them went inside, and the other half took up posts around the portico as the doors were swung shut. From the sacred atrium, the music of a threnody sung in five voices sounded, echoing eerily from the stones. Song, Penric was reminded, was considered an especially acceptable offering to the gods, being a gift of pure spirit. The people in the portico did not disperse, but rather, settled as if preparing for a long wait. Penric couldn't guess if this was good, giving a crowd to blend into, or bad, the extra watchmen having leisure to survey the scene and decide the strangers on the far bench didn't belong here.

After a long, frustrating silence, Nikys finally said, "I'm going to find out what's going on." She unfolded and donned her respectable dark green widow's cloak, and made for the portico. Adelis and Penric both twitched, but really, the gathering remained tame enough, and Nikys was the least memorable intelligencer among them. She spent what seemed to Penric quite a long time chatting with other women on the periphery of the spectators. Finally, she trod back, a dark discreet shape in the fire-limned shadows. At her gesture, the two men slid apart, and she sat down between them with a sigh.

"They're going to be at this all night," she reported. "It's a double funeral for a double suicide. Rather a tragedy. Two young people from a pair of feuding families fell in love and, not allowed to be together in life, decided to be together in death."

"Seems idiotic," said Adelis. Penric, tactfully, did not bring up how recently Adelis had been considering such an exit from his own dark woes.

Nikys shrugged, not disagreeing. "It appears they were very young. Anyway, the magistrates and the Sosie divines ordered both families to pray all night for their souls, and for atonement for their strife. By morning, people expect there to be either a reconciliation, or blood on the temple floor and no survivors, and it didn't sound as if the magistrates much cared which by this time."

"Well." Adelis rubbed his neck. "We can't sleep in there, then." He frowned. "And I won't have Nikys sleep on the street."

Penric agreed with that. His own preference was to scout out a high place to hole up. Desdemona lent him the ability to see in the dark, so that wasn't going to be much worse for him than such a search by daylight, but getting the other two up after him, and in stealthy silence, was going to be tricky. The night was moonless, making the narrow lanes pitch black in most places. All the good citizens would be indoors by this time, leaving mainly the other sort abroad. Granted, any villain unwittingly tackling a Temple-trained sorcerer could be in for a horrible surprise, and he doubted Adelis would make easy prey, either. But it would be far better to slip in and out of Sosie without any incident at all.

Thank you, murmured Desdemona, within him.

Aye. Cedonia was a beautiful country, Pen thought, but it kept trying to kill him. At some point, his demon might not be able to keep up, and then they...no, *she* would be in real trouble. His troubles would be over, presumably.

But they weren't over yet. He hoisted himself up and led his charges into the dark and winding passages, the paving stones usually dry underfoot but sometimes unpleasantly not. He held Nikys's hand, and she held Adelis's, so he was able to guide them safely around the worst of the hazards. The houses here were in the Cedonian style of high blank walls around inner courtyards, the few street-facing windows or balconies confined to upper stories. No handy stairs, or ladders, or even climbing vines rewarded his investigations.

You shouldn't be trying to climb yet anyway, Des muttered in disapproval. *You might get dizzy again. No sprinting, either.*

I'm feeling stronger now. Chest's stopped hurting. You do excellent work.

Flattery will not avail you, she responded not entirely truthfully, part placated, part still stern.

Orange light flickered at the next corner. Penric poked his head cautiously around. The light had two sources: a simple candle lantern hanging on a bracket above a doorway, and a brighter oil lantern held by one of a pair of soldiers. Young officers, Penric guessed by their dress and demeanor, captains or lieutenants of hundreds; Adelis would be able to tell at a glance. The other soldier pounded impatiently on the stout wooden door.

"Hoy! Open up, Zihre! Don't leave your best customers standing in the street!"

More pounding. At last the door creaked, and a woman thrust her head out. "We're not open, gentlemen. Come back another night."

"Oh, you can let us in, surely," wheedled the officer. A bit drunk, Pen guessed.

"We're closed for washing. Unless you want to scrub laundry, be off with you."

"All that hot steam could be exciting," the drunken officer allowed, attempting to grab and kiss her. She evaded him without effort or apparent offense.

"Yes, we could hold your head under the suds till you grow smarter," she returned. "Or cleaner. Whichever happens first." His companion guffawed. "If you're not the laundresses"—she leaned out and looked up and down the street—"I can't accommodate you tonight."

A bit more whining left the woman unmoved, and the pair gave up and left. Their voices sounded again at the next corner, a lewd joke and a sharp rejoinder. An older woman, trailed by two others carrying sacks, rejected their inebriated attentions and made for the light, under which the lady of the house, seeing them approach, had paused.

"Ah, good." The woman in the entryway waved and beckoned. "At last."

The presumed-laundress held out her hand to halt her companions. "Yes, we're here, at this unholy hour. But I'm telling you straight out, Zihre, it's double pay tonight or we're not coming in. And your girls can boil their own crawly sheets." She mimed an exaggerated shudder.

Zihre sighed. "Yes, yes, whatever it takes. We can't do business at all till this Bastard-sent plague is eradicated." She tapped her lips with her thumb in a quick averting half-prayer, as if the god himself might be listening, offended at this scorning of His ambiguous gifts.

Penric, rapidly figuring out the situation, grinned to himself. *Bastard be praised indeed.* He whispered to Adelis and Nikys, "Wait here. I may be able to win us shelter for the night." He raised his chin and strode forward, ignoring Nikys's *What?* and Adelis's *We can't take Nikys in there!*

"Madame Zihre?" he called in his most dulcet tones, as she made to pull the door closed again behind the party of stumping, grumping laundresses.

"I'm sorry, sir, we're closed tonight," she began perfunctorily as Penric stepped forward into the light of her door lantern. She looked up into his face, and her eyes widened. "So very, very sorry!"

He smiled back with all his heart. Prostitutes, after all, were numbered among the Bastard's own flock. Along with pirates, Pen supposed, but he didn't think he'd deal well with the latter, oath-sworn divine or not. "Ah. I didn't come to employ, but to seek employment. May I come in and speak further?"

She blinked. "We've not kept lads for the loves of the Bastard before, but that's not to say we might not start. Are you experienced? Not that you'd need to be, necessarily. I could train you." The corners of her mouth crept up.

Penric cleared his throat, to block Desdemona's knowing snicker. "Ah, ha, not that sort of employment. I am given to understand you are troubled with an unfortunate outbreak of personal parasites. I've had experience eradicating such pests before, at houses such as this. I am a Temple sorcerer, Learned...Jurald." He signed himself, forehead-lips-navel-groin-heart for the tally of the five gods, and tapped his lips again for the Bastard's special blessing.

Her dark eyes grew shrewd. She was a decidedly handsome older woman, Pen saw at this closer range. Her dress was more dignified than provocative, aside from a wide green belt at her waist, glimmering with sewn pearls, that supported her bodice in an attractive manner. "You are too pretty to be Learned Anybody," she protested.

"I could make you a scholarly argument, but really, I think it would be faster for me to simply demonstrate my skills. And you can judge for yourself." He kept up the blinding smile. "If I cannot perform to your satisfaction, you will owe me nothing."

"And what would I owe you if you did?"

"No great price, merely shelter for myself and my two"—he made a rapid recalculation—"servants for the night. We've found ourselves unexpectedly benighted in Sosie without the, er, resources we expected to receive here, and must make do."

Her eyes narrowed back down. "Why not go to the Temple, then, oh learned divine?" Unkempt on her doorstep, dressed and probably also smelling like a farm laborer, there was certainly nothing of the divine about him.

"It's a long story." Which he had better make up as soon as possible. "There was a shipwreck involved," he essayed, and then realized he had a better one. "The Sosie Temple, as you may know, is much occupied tonight with settling a tragic feud between two local families."

"Oh," she said. "Yes. That. Young fools. Although the old fools were the worse." She snorted. "I won't say they got what they deserved, because no one deserves to lose their child, but it's to be hoped they've learned a lesson from the gods that they refused from anyone else. Everyone in town was tired of their riot and rumpus." She gave way and opened her door.

Penric thanked her, and hurried back to collect Nikys and Adelis.

"I'm a traveling sorcerer-divine, you two are my servants, and we were recently shipwrecked...somewhere," he whispered in rapid tutorial. "Which is why we have no baggage or money. I've just undertaken to rid the house of an infestation of, er, insect pests, in exchange for a night's lodging."

"What kind of pests?" asked Nikys.

Adelis said, repressively, "Bedbugs."

"Oh? From the way she was talking with the laundress, I'd have guessed crab lice."

Penric choked down Desdemona's laugh as Nikys sailed past him. "Could be both, but I can be the bane of either. Remember, you are servants.

Tired, quiet servants. A guard and a maid. Who keep to themselves."

"You have the first part right," Adelis growled, following her. "Shipwreck? You do know we're eighty miles inland, yes?"

"We had a long walk," Pen returned, swallowing aggravation. Adelis might resent being cast again as an actor, but a guardsman should be less of a stretch for him than a widow. If he deigned to cooperate.

Crossing the threshold, Penric signed himself again, and murmured, "Five gods bless and keep this house safe from all harm." *And us as well.* Their hostess's fine plucked eyebrows twitched up at the gesture, a tiny concession to belief in his self-proclaimed calling.

She turned, took up a pole with a hook from its wall bracket, and used it to retrieve the lantern over the door before closing it again with a firm thud, setting the bar across. "That's served its purpose," she murmured. "Our porter's job, but he's busy hauling water just now." She motioned her new guests after her.

The house may well have belonged to a rich family, before falling to its present purpose. Spacious, but short of palatial. The arrangement, Penric saw as they followed Zihre inside, was typical of this country: stone-built, an entry atrium with a mosaic floor, then a larger atrium also with a second floor of rooms built around it on a gallery. A small walled garden beyond held a separate outbuilding for the kitchen, laundry, and bathhouse. The garden boasted its own well, and a stream of activity as people carried water and wood for the boiling vats, under the stern direction of the laundresses. The general air was cranky and harried. And itchy. Not the sort of evening party that usually graced this garden, Penric imagined.

Hopelessly the diagnostician, Penric asked, "When did your current troubles commence, do you know?"

Zihre shrugged. "Perhaps a month ago. It was either a party of merchants, or some new soldiers from the barracks. Which means the boys will doubtless be gifting them back to us."

Adelis winced, no doubt able to picture the military side of the scene. Penric wondered if he should pass on some tips for diplomatically delousing her customers that he'd picked up back in Martensbridge, when he had been asked out as a physician-sorcerer to take care of a similar plague in certain establishments there. That had started an extraordinary education for him, to be sure, the like of which he could never have imagined back in his canton mountain boyhood. He'd made many new and interesting friends. And come to better know the courtesan Mira of Adria, the image of his demon's long-dead fifth rider who lived, in a sense, along with the rest of her strange sisterhood inside his head. He suspected he'd be asking her for advice again soon.

External parasites did not require nearly the delicacy to dispose of as internal ones. He and Des were so practiced by now he could likely do it with a simple stroll around the premises, but he supposed he'd better make enough of a show that their hostess would realize he'd done anything at all, and credit him for it. Rather the reverse of his usual preference for discretion. They were going to need the credit. Really, when he had time someday he needed to work out a way to make his magics visible at need to ungifted observers, some sort of sham light show perhaps. Maybe the marketplace jongleurs would have some tricks he could adapt.

Penric, Des murmured. *Take a look at this.*

His outer vision was abruptly flooded with his inner one, and he glanced around, wondering if she had spotted a sundered ghost. The lingering smudges of those lost souls were common enough that he usually had Des spare him the distraction, lest he alarm companions by constantly dodging around things they could not see. But at his sight's fullest intensity he also saw the souls of those still alive, congruent with their bodies in an eerie swirling nimbus of life and light. It seemed to him such intimate god-sight ought not to be gifted to a mere man, but he'd learned to use it back when he'd been a practicing physician. Far too much practice, but it hadn't made perfect. Right now, Adelis was mostly dark red, stress and anger well-contained, no contradictions there. Annoying as it sometimes was, Pen appreciated the man's straightforwardness. Nikys—he sneaked a peek—was blue with weariness, a snarled thread of thick green worry running through that he quite wanted to wind out of her, if only he had a way, which he didn't.

No, said Des. *Look at Madame Zihre. Left breast.*

She was a normal mix of colors, more to the blue and green, but he saw at once the black blot of chaos

riding in her breast. That familiar, lethal egg... *Oh.*
He gulped. *Oh, Des, I wish you hadn't shown me
that.* Which was the *other* reason he avoided using
his inner sight. All that overwhelming pain, pour-
ing in from the people around him—how did gods
and saints endure such knowledge?

The tumor's still encapsulated. There's a chance.
Des let the disrupting visions fade, to Pen's relief.
*Or I should not have troubled you. Attend to her
later, perhaps.*

Perhaps. Pen drew breath and forced his attention back to his external surroundings. Madame
Zihre frowned doubtfully at Pen's companions,
following in behind them—Nikys with their sack
of meager belongings and Penric's medical case,
Adelis, his hat pulled down again, clutching a roll
that looked exactly like a bundle of weapons.

"Could we take my servants to our chamber,
first?" Penric suggested. "They're very tired."

"Mm, yes," said Zihre thoughtfully. She
plucked a candlestick from a table by the stairs, lit
it from another, and led them up to the small gallery over the entry atrium. Entering a bedchamber
there, she shared the flame with a brace of candles on a shelf, and a couple in fine mirrored wall

sconces, and gave Penric a sidelong glance. "How about this?"

The place had a rumpled air; after a quick survey, Des reported, *Lively in here. She's testing you.*

"Is it...clean?" asked Nikys, pausing on the threshold in doubt.

Penric waved a hand, and enjoyed the familiar little flush of warmth through his body as Des divested chaos. "It is now."

"Ah. Thank you, Learned Jurald." Getting into her assigned role at once, hah. She smiled and entered confidently, Adelis trailing.

By the bemused purse of her lips, Zihre was more persuaded by Nikys's belief than by Penric's patter.

Nikys set down the case and hefted the sack stuffed with their clothing, mostly filthy by now. "May I join your laundresses, Madame? What little we saved from the wreck is overdue a washing in something other than seawater."

"Certainly. Come down when you're ready."

A female voice shrilly calling Zihre's name echoed from the atrium, and she grimaced.

"We'll follow you shortly," Penric told her, and she nodded and hurried off to address her next household crisis.

Penric shut the door behind her. A basin and ewer sat on the chamber's washstand; he seized the moment to splash his face and hands, saying to Nikys and Adelis, "Adelis should stay out of sight in this room. We'd best get our story straight. Where did our ship wreck?"

"Cape Crow would make the most sense," allowed Adelis.

"Right, so I coasted down from, say, Trigonie. Trying to get around to"—Penric mentally reviewed the map—"Thasalon. After the wreck, I wouldn't get on a ship again, nor would any captain have me, because of those nautical superstitions about sorcerers aboard being bad luck."

"Apparently confirmed," Adelis murmured.

Penric ignored this. "So we struck west overland. You two have not been with me for long. Which should allow you to say *I don't know* to most questions about me."

"You hired us in Trigonie," offered Nikys, entering into the spirit of this. "We worked cheaply, because we were trying to get home to Cedonia. Should we still be a man and his wife?"

"You've been that for the last while. Better change it around. Go back to brother and sister?"

Nikys, kneeling to sort dirty clothing, nodded.

Adelis folded his arms and looked skeptical. "Why are you traveling?"

"Temple business," Penric returned at once. "Which, of course, I have not discussed with you. You think I'm a..."

"Spy?" said Nikys brightly.

"Lunatic?" suggested Adelis.

"Called as a physician," Penric suppressed this flight of fancy, or commentary. "To treat someone important. Or moderately important, I suppose. But, really, if you just say *Temple business* and look down your nose at your interrogator, it usually suffices."

Adelis's lips twitched. "Confirming something I've long suspected about Temple functionaries."

Penric waved this off, and bent to help Nikys with her now-sorted bundles.

"No." She tapped his hands away. "No lifting for you till Des says."

"I'm doing much better," Penric protested, but rose empty-handed. "Though I'd as soon get this night's work over with as swiftly as possible. I'm about dead on my feet. Not literally," he added hastily, as Nikys looked up in alarm.

Adelis hoisted her up, and the bundles into her arms, and opened the door for them.

"I'll try to bring us back some food," she told him.

"Don't trip on the stairs," Adelis called after them in an under-voice. "Or Penric's tongue."

PENRIC CAUGHT up with Madame Zihre downstairs, and had her guide him around her house from room to room. The place was surprisingly free of bedbugs, but while he was at it he had Des strip out in passing endemic fleas, flies, wool moths, and all their eggs, from every cranny, cupboard, chest, and fold of fabric, as well as his primary target of lice. Nearly the entire household was collected in the garden and laundry, aiding the washing, which allowed him to stand in the shadows and divest them all more-or-less at once. *Heartwarming*, Des quipped happily, growing replete with balance. Pen dissuaded Madame Zihre from introducing him, or even letting him be seen by his beneficiaries, as he was beginning to evolve a new idea.

Leaning against an atrium pillar in the shadows with his arms folded, he remarked to her, "You, happily, are not infested."

"You can tell this?" Her expression had not shifted much from its initial dubiousness. Like any merchant, she'd likely had plenty of experience with cheaters and charlatans, and was plainly waiting for him to slip up in some revealing way.

He nodded. "Is there someplace we can go to talk quietly?"

Her lips drew back in a half-smile, dryly satisfied, as she braced for whatever sly pitch she now expected from him. "Come this way."

She led him upstairs into a bedroom, richly appointed and obviously her own, and unlocked a door to a small private cabinet. A writing table, quills and inkpots, shelves with ledgers for accounts and tax records, a strongbox—this was her real personal space. She lit the generous candles and settled him on a stool crowded by the wall, turning around the straight chair at the table for herself.

Penric clasped his hands between his knees, smiling to conceal his own unhappiness. He had *so* not wanted to be drawn into this calling again...

"Madame Zihre. Do you know what rides in your left breast?"

She gasped, her hand flying to the spot. *Aye, she knows*, murmured Des.

She swallowed and raised her chin, and said in a voice gone grim, "My death. In due course. Such a curse killed my older sister…eventually."

Penric could picture it all too well. He nodded. "I made acquaintance with such things when I was training as a sorcerer-physician in, ah, my home country. I had no luck destroying any tumors that had spread like tree roots, but if they were still encapsulated like an egg, sometimes…I did." But less luck persuading his fellow physicians in Martensbridge, or the patients they brought too late before him, of the critical differences, visible only to him.

"How, destroy?"

"Small, repeated applications of heat, of burning, inside the affected flesh. Although lately I have bethought that burning with cold would be a gentler method."

"Burn with cold?" She stared at him. "That sounds mad."

"Ah, Cedonia is a warm country. I keep forgetting. Yes, it is possible to burn with cold." He sat back, held up his fingers, and concentrated. A tiny hailstone grew from the air between them. He let it enlarge for several breaths, till it was the size of a pullet egg, and held it out to Madame Zihre.

She took the ice lump, and her lips parted in surprise. It was the first visible, uphill magic he had worked in front of her. When she looked up at him again, her expression was frighteningly intense, shock and fear and hope intermingled, and a whole new kind of doubt. "Oh," she breathed. "You really *are*. You seem so young."

He nodded, not bothering to feign an offense he did not feel. "I'm thirty, but never mind. Do you wish me to try to treat you?"

Her eyes narrowed and her lips thinned again, as she thought she spotted the hook. "What is your price?"

"For this, nothing," said Penric. "Not least because—and you have to understand this—I cannot guarantee you will be healed, or that the tumor will not return. They did, sometimes." And often worse than before, destroying false hopes as devastatingly as a fire. "My offer stands regardless. Nevertheless, I do have a need. I want to travel on from Sosie as someone else, unrecognizable. My servants also."

She took this in, blinking thoughtfully. "Why such secrecy?"

"Temple business." Not wholly a lie. The arch-divine of Adria had assigned him to his duke, who had assigned him to fetch General Arisaydia, and things had spun out—of control, among other things—from there. Bringing him, all unplanned, here. Unplanned by any human schemer, anyway, he conceded uneasily.

You know, for a divine of the god of lies, you cleave to the truth rather closely, Des commented.

It's the scholar in me. Hush.

But Madame Zihre, for all her wariness, accepted this without demur, awarding him a slightly more respectful nod. "So...what is it that you do for such things?" She motioned to her breast once more.

"As you have observed, the deepest magics never show above the surface. It would be helpful for my precision if I may touch you."

"Right now?" She seemed to expect more preparation. More ceremony, something.

He was too tired to invent any. "Soonest begun." *Soonest done.* He opened his hand toward her. "I should warn you, you will feel some pain."

"Well, that's some proof, isn't it?" She shrugged out of half her bodice with an almost medical unselfconsciousness, a curious parallel between their respective crafts, and leaned toward him.

Des, sight, please. The inner vision came up at once. He placed his fingers on her fine soft skin, found the dark blot, and called up the spot of sucking cold in its center as he had just done for the hailstone. Her breath caught as she felt it, but she held still as the chill increased, though her hands gripped her skirts on her knees. She was not the first woman he'd met who endured dire pain in disturbing silence, and he wondered if Nikys would be another such. When the ice reached the edge of the blot, he stopped and sat back.

She inhaled, and allowed herself to pant. "That's all?"

"First treatment. I should repeat it tomorrow, to be sure. As sure as I can be. Then later I'll need to open it and drain the killed matter, to prevent necrosis and infection." And cram the area with as much uphill magic as he could make it accept, but that part would be invisible to her.

She nodded and reordered her clothing. Her breathing was slowing, to his relief. "I can feel it. Maybe it's doing me good."

"It will likely swell and hurt worse through the night. Tell me everything you feel. It will help me…" *To guess what I've done* was perhaps not the most reassuring thing to say. He left the sentence hanging.

"So…how do you plan to make yourself unrecognizable, and how do you imagine I can help? Can't you do it by magic?"

"Sorcery only works that way in tales, to my regret. I would love to be able to turn myself into a bird and fly, wouldn't you? I cannot even manage a cloak of invisibility, but I've found it's possible to manage a cloak of misdirection." He took a breath. "I think it will be best to start from the skin out. Have you, anywhere about your premises, a woman's undergarment that used to be called a *bum roll?*"

"Oh!" She looked him up and down, and her face lit with true delight for the first time since he'd met her. "Oh, yes. I see what you have in mind. …Oh, I *do* adore a masquerade."

III

WHEN THE UPROAR of the nighttime laundering and bathing crisis had died away, and nearly all the linens and garments of the household were strung on lines across the garden to await the morning sun, Nikys sneaked a bath for herself before returning to their room. She found Penric leaning on the balcony railing outside their door, looking pensive, though he straightened and smiled when he saw her. "Adelis fell asleep," he told her. "He's really not as recovered yet as he thinks he is."

Nikys wondered if that went for Penric as well; he looked exhausted. She entered the chamber quietly, calculating how they were to divide the bed this time. But she found Madame Zihre had sent up two pallets for the traveling divine's retainers. Adelis already occupied one of them.

"You should take the bed," Penric whispered.

"No, you should," she whispered back. "What if someone comes in? It would look strange to have given it up to your maidservant."

He opened his mouth, but she held her finger to his lips and shook her head. He glanced at Adelis and forbore to continue the argument, to her relief. Her pallet was still an improvement over a pile of straw. They had surely not reached safety yet. But with Adelis snoring on one side, and the gentle creaks of Penric nesting himself into the bed on the other, it seemed a sufficient substitute that all her anxieties failed to keep her awake long.

This was not a household that rose with the dawn the way her well-ordered and much-missed villa in Patos had. But it was not long after first light that a quiet tap announced a servant with wash water and a bit of breakfast for the odd guests. Nikys intercepted it at the door, and swapped out the chamber pot. They gratefully devoured the hot tea, bread, and fruit. Nikys was surprised when the next knock was not the returning servant, but the lady of the house herself.

"Learned Jurald. My bathhouse is temporarily deserted. This is a good moment to begin that task we discussed last night."

"I should be pleased, Madame," Penric replied smoothly.

"Bring your maidservant. I don't want to get my hands all over henna."

They all shuffled after her, through the forest of laundry already half-dry in the day's promise of heat, to the little bathhouse, where Adelis was induced to haul water on the promise that he could be next. He frowned over his shoulder as he was sent off to stay out of sight till then.

Penric shucked off the shirt he'd slept in and started to untie his trousers, then stopped. "Oh. I did not mean to offend your modesty, Madame Khatai. After four years of teaching anatomy to the apprentices, I'm afraid anyone with their skin still on looks dressed to me."

Even Zihre raised her eyebrows at this rueful comment.

Nikys took this in. *Urk.* He wasn't worrying about the other madame's modesty, she noted. "Learned," she sighed, "just get in the bath."

"Ah. Right."

He was sluiced—Nikys stood on the bench to lift the bucket high enough—soaped himself up, sluiced again, and then nipped delicately into the wooden tub. Thin he was, but strappy, not scrawny, she was pleased to note. And that milk skin went all over.

And then she was allowed to fulfill the fantasy that she would not have confessed aloud under threat of thumbscrews, and wash that amazing hair. This was followed with a light henna rinse, which almost broke her heart to apply. But the silver-blond transmuted to an almost equally entrancing copper-blond, not raw red the way the color sometimes came out. Zihre handed him a thin robe after he'd dried himself, and Nikys made him squeeze his brilliant eyes shut and very carefully colored his eyebrows as well. Her hands emerged a somewhat less-attractive orange.

Zihre smiled in satisfaction. "Ah, yes. Very natural. I thought that might do."

"It's better than the walnut dye I started this trip with. I believe it will be best not to overexaggerate anything."

"It's a start. That beard stubble must go, next. Did you bring your own razor, or shall we use one of ours?"

It occurred to Nikys then that for all she'd seen Penric shave Adelis, during his blindness, she'd never seen him shave himself, even in the constant close quarters they'd shared on their flight.

"I actually have a trick for that. A bit of oil and a cloth will suffice."

He rubbed oil over his jaw, then scrubbed it thoroughly with the cloth. The stubble—miraculously—seemed to have transferred to the cloth. Was that uphill magic, or down? Nikys tensed as Zihre ran her hand over the smoothed skin so revealed.

"My word. *That's* effective." She gestured down his chest, faintly dusted with fine gold hairs. "And now the rest of it."

"Er. I had actually planned to keep my clothes on." He waved a wiry arm. "Long sleeves. High neck. And so on. A look of expensive reserve."

"We'll have to experiment with the clothes. I don't have much of that style. The upper half of your chest, then."

He grimaced, but complied. And it began to dawn on Nikys that it wasn't just his hair color he was planning to change for a new disguise. "Are you proposing to set my brother an example in acting, Learned?"

"Something like that. We'll see if it works."

His back being turned just then, she tapped her upcurving lips in a prayer of heartfelt gratitude to the Bastard. And when Zihre said, "We can continue this privately in my chamber," picked up after them like a proper maidservant and followed with zeal.

She collected Penric's smallclothes off the line in passing, threadbare linen trews almost dry, and, when the door of Zihre's chamber closed behind them, handed them silently across. Penric gave her a smile of thanks and slipped them on at once.

Zihre's…workshop, Nikys decided to think of it, was nicely appointed; part, no doubt, of keeping her prices up. Nikys had a shrewd guess of just how much coin it cost to run a household with a dozen employees and a dozen more servants, with nightly hospitality added atop. The cleanliness, recently restored, and the pleasant effects of the decorations no doubt helped as well to keep the house's customers from growing too rowdy, striking a fine balance between inviting and daunting. The furnishings were for the most part simple, storage chests and a wider-than-usual bed. The one personal grace-note was a large collection of masquerade masks arrayed on one wall, inventively decorated.

The bed was stacked with women's dresses and undergarments. Zihre had Penric stand while she held up one and then another against his long body, murmuring, *No, no...yes, no,* and tossing them onto alternate piles. She shook out two extended tubes of stuffed cloth; Penric pointed without hesitation at the thinner. "Hm, yes. I thought those snake-hips would need more, but you're right." She fitted its strings around his waist, so that the tube fell to and circled his hips. Another wrap went around his upper torso, and they debated how much stuffing to stick in it; again, choosing less not more.

"Your hands and feet need work. It's the details that do the job, you know."

"Indeed, Madame." Cheerfully obedient to her pointing, he sat himself on the bench in front of a small table with drawers and a mirror.

She dove into the drawers and unearthed several lacquered boxes, full of more grooming tools and makeup than Nikys had ever seen collected together. Zihre set Nikys to work on Penric's feet, and herself tackled his hands. Such a pedicure was not a task Nikys had undertaken for another person since before she'd married, trading services with like-minded girlfriends, giggling together as they clumsily copied the skills of mothers and older sisters. Well, and the care she had tried to give Kymis, in his later illness, but that had entailed no giggling. By the little smile playing about Zihre's lips, Nikys wondered if she, too, had fond memories of such youthful hen parties.

Penric's feet were hard-used. But the routines of files and scrubs and oils came back to her soon enough, aided by a few workwomanlike tips from Zihre. The bright copper nail lacquer that Zihre handed off to her finished the job, and she sat back, pleased, to find Penric looking down at her with a crooked half-smile. She had not the least clue what he—he and Desdemona, never forget—were thinking of all this.

"Hair's dry now," said Zihre, fluffing it; the henna had caused it to curl more than its usual soft waves. "What do you think? Back? Up?" She rolled the mass of ruddy silk in her hands and twisted it this way and that.

"Down, surely," put in Penric, rolling his eyes up in a vain attempt to see what she was about. "To screen my neck as much as possible."

"Mm, but one wants to make the most of those cheekbones." Combs and clips in her clever hands split the difference, resulting in a handful of wisps falling across Penric's forehead, hair from the sides drawn up to a knot at the crown, and a copper cascade falling free down his nape.

"Now let's see..." Zihre's hands dove into her makeup box. She inked his lashes brown, was dissuaded from applying more than a hint of kohl to his lids, and finished with a mere brush of rouge to his cheeks and lips. For the first time, Penric twisted around to check the results in the little mirror, his henna'd eyebrows quirking.

"Stand." Zihre gestured and Penric complied. She shook out a loose length of blue-green dyed linen and dropped it over his head, careful not to muss the hair. After guiding his copper-tipped hands through the sleeves, she smoothed the soft folds down. The sleeves were pieced and pierced along the top edges, allowing pale skin to peek through, holding the sea-colored cloth demurely draped across his collarbones; it dipped lower in the back, veiled by his hair.

The hem, unfortunately, only fell to his calves. Nikys pointed mutely.

"Yes, I thought that might be the case. Here, girl, help me." They collaborated on pinning a second skirt, a darker blue with a ruffled hem, around the roll at his hips and under the dress, which made up, or down, the requisite length to his ankles. A belt of copper links cinching the waist finished the job. Zihre stood back to study her handiwork, lips pursed. Penric blinked back, amiably.

"Five gods," murmured Nikys. "That's really unfair."

"Amen," agreed Zihre, with a vast sigh.

"What?" said Penric, as the contemplative silence lingered.

"Never mind, Learned." Zihre turned and rummaged in another chest, retrieving a pair of clogs raised more in the heel than the ball of the foot. "Try these on."

Doubtfully, he sat. "Wouldn't flat sandals be better? Surely I am already too tall."

"Goddesses are permitted to tower." She tapped his pink cheek. "More to the point, it will change your walk. No use in adorning you like this if the body inside still lurches about like a lad."

After a moment, he nodded agreement, and Nikys knelt to adjust the leather straps, careful not to smudge her lacquer-work. He rose again to teeter cautiously around the room. He muttered something in Adriac.

"What was that, Learned?" said Nikys.

"Mira says she used to risk her neck in shoes three times this high, on cobbled streets with the canals waiting for a misstep, and that I shouldn't be such a weakling." On the second pass around the room he was steadier; on the third, natural, and she wondered what swift tutorials his multi-minded demon was offering him.

"And what is this tall and elegant red-haired lady's name and history, Learned?" Nikys asked. "Not to mention that of her servants?" There had been such a rapid succession of tales to account for themselves, she was losing track.

"Ah. Good question."

He headed for the bench; Zihre put in, "Don't *plunk*. Dispose of your skirts gracefully."

He hesitated, then did so quite credibly. "I suppose I had better be Mira. That will be easiest to remember. History...hm. I don't know how long this masquerade must last."

To the border of Orbas, quite possibly, Nikys imagined. How many days? And they still had no money.

After a moment's thought, Penric offered, "I am Mira of Adria, a...retiring courtesan of that realm.

Traveling to private service. In our youth, Zihre and I were friends—no, better, we had a mutual friend. We have not met before. In her name, I imposed upon your hospitality when my party was unexpectedly benighted in Sosie. Because, hm, why did we lose our baggage this time...?"

"You sent it by carter," Zihre suggested, "and it has not arrived. In fact, it may never arrive."

"Oh, very good."

"It happens," she sighed. "Lost in a river crossing, they claimed, but *I* think it was stolen." Nikys wasn't sure if this was an addition to their fiction, or a personal anecdote. It certainly sounded more plausible than shipwreck, and much less interesting, thus needing far fewer supporting details.

"And your servants?" Nikys prodded Penric.

"Have not been with me long, but share my destination."

"And my brother's...?" She touched the upper half of her face. Penric gave her a fractional shrug, acknowledging the problem. Any halfway-accurate description of the fugitives circulating by now must mention Adelis's burn scars, unique and condemning. The old masquerade mask that they had modified for him back in Patos to hold his dressings in place was no solution; too obvious a disguise, it would draw the attention of observers just as dangerously as the disfigurement itself. Her eye fell on the collection of fine masks decorating Zihre's wall, and an idea began to niggle at her. *Later.*

Penric—Mira—tapped his, or her, lips with a thumb. He glanced up through his lashes at Madame Zihre. "I should like to repeat my treatment of last night, now. How did you fare by this morning?"

"Sore and swollen, as you said." She shrugged. "Not...unbearable. Is it time again?"

He gave a tiny nod. "There is a balance to be struck between destruction and healing. I provide the destruction, but your own body must provide the healing. Mostly." The rather merry mood between them had suddenly turned sober, and Nikys's brows drew down.

To Nikys's brief bewilderment, though she had the wits not to betray it, Zihre knelt before him and composedly undid her bodice. Penric frowned and laid two fingers upon her left breast at a patch indeed swollen and reddish, and his face fell into that look of inward concentration that Nikys had learned to mark when he'd been healing Adelis's eyes. She bit her lip. Wasn't he supposed to be saving Desdemona's strained powers for his own bruised heart, right now? She must tax him later on that.

Zihre's breath caught, and she went rigidly still for a minute, until Penric's hand fell away.

"Still bearable?" he asked gently.

She nodded and rose, looking down at him with that worried mystification he so often engendered in people.

"I'll fetch in my medical case to you later and attend to the draining, and then we'll see," he said.

Another chin-dip.

"I should prefer not to impose upon you any longer than we must," Penric went on.

She waved a hand. "This morning's amusement repays me for a few baths and meals, Learned Jurald. Or—Lady Mira? Madame Mira?"

"Sora Mira, if we are to go by the Adriac style." He pondered. "I must work on my accent. Her accent. Mira spoke little Cedonian. Excellent Darthacan, though. How is my voice, by the way?" He repeated in a higher register, "How is this voice?"

"Don't overdo," advised Zihre. "Tall Mira can be throaty. Or breathy. Just don't go deep, or loud."

"Understood." He started to stand up, paused, and rose with more conscious grace. "Well. Let us make a test." He smiled at Nikys. "Shall we go introduce Sora Mira to your brother?"

Nikys barely controlled her grin, struggling for servility. "Oh, yes *please*, Learned."

Madame Zihre waved them out, turning to restore the tools of her trade to their boxes, and Nikys and Penric exited to the atrium balcony.

"Let's go around a time or two," Penric muttered. "I need to practice this walk."

Nikys nodded, and he laced his arm through hers to stroll along. After a moment, she asked, "What were you doing for Madame Zihre, just then? When you laid on your hand?"

He grimaced. "Just a little healing. I hope."

"What sort? Uphill or down?"

"Some of both. She suffers from a tumor there. Not a tame sort, I'm afraid."

"Oh." She hesitated. "You can do this?"

"Sometimes. Sometimes not." He sighed. "I suppose we will be long gone before it has time to prove not."

"Is it costly to you? Magically?"

He waved away the question, a non-answer that made her suspicious. He lowered his voice. "Not as costly as the risk to Zihre of harboring fugitives, even if unknowingly. If things go ill."

"Well." She drew breath. "We should not let them go ill, then."

"Aye." His voice fell softer still. "I should have been able to understand such things better, back in Martensbridge. Tumors and their ilk. There is an element of chaos involved, that I can sense direct, but no prayer addressed to my god ever returned any useful insight. Despite the fact that several of my demon's first human riders eventually died of related disorders. Including Mira, come to think."

"We are sorry," said Desdemona, even more quietly. "We did not realize, then."

He gave a curiously compassionate nod. "Not your fault, exactly. It couldn't have been until Umelan—Des's sixth rider," he added aside to Nikys, "fell into the hands of the Bastard's Order in Brajar that you even could learn to balance your chaos, and not to shed it internally unawares." He ducked his head to Nikys again. "Which is yet another cause for the Temple to pursue hedge sorcerers and secure them to its disciplines, I suppose. Or else divest them of their demons. Not a reason that is widely known or understood."

Desdemona vented a tiny growl at the mention of the Temple's demonic destructions, but did not press the argument. Nikys gave the arm wrapped in hers a little squeeze, and she was not sure which of the occupants of that complicated head she was attempting to console. Was Penric at any such inner risk now? It didn't sound as if he thought so.

They fetched up at their chamber door. "Why is it, I wonder," Penric mused, "that men dressed as women seem more risible than women dressed as men?"

Nikys shook her head. "I don't really know. It doesn't seem fair, does it?" She poked glumly at her well-filled bodice. "I don't suppose it's an experiment worth my time to try. Not since I was twelve. Not even with tight wraps."

"No. Definitely not worth your time. Or your worry. You're perfect as you are." A faint smile curved his rose-tinted lips. "At least Des likes the gown. I don't know how an incorporeal demon should have developed a taste for fine clothing, but she has. At home I try to do my best by her, within the limits of my calling and purse, but evidently she's missed the styles of her own sex." Penric took a moment to compose himself, in both senses, as Mira, then gestured Nikys ahead of him.

Adelis had used the bathhouse while she and Penric had been so long occupied in Zihre's chamber, and was dressed again in his least-smelly shirt and trousers, barefoot. Nikys reminded herself to go collect the rest of their laundered clothes off the line soon. As Penric wafted in behind her, the startled Adelis grabbed his hat, tipped it low over his forehead, and stood up. He shot Nikys a glare of dismay.

"I'm sorry, is this your room?" he managed. "Madame Zihre assigned it to—to my master."

"More or less, but that's fine." Mira cast him a dazzling smile. "I don't mind sharing."

"I met a new friend," said Nikys brightly. "Her name is Mira."

Adelis scowled. "You shouldn't be chattering with people out there. Learned...Jurald told us to be discreet."

"Please, sit," Mira said throatily, waving a kind, pale hand. "I didn't mean to interrupt your work."

Adelis, who hadn't been doing any, looked around as if for some task to feign, found none, and sank back into his chair. Mira sashayed to the bed and sat with a cheery seductive bounce, arms back to support herself, chest thrust out. She tilted her head, somehow making her blue eyes seem to glint like sun on the sea. "I met your sister in the laundry. I do love travelers' tales." She kicked a rather long copper-tipped foot against her ruffled skirt hem.

"What tales have you been telling?" Adelis asked Nikys. His attempted-casual tone did not quite mask alarm. Really, with his hat pulled down like that this might not be wholly a fair test.

"You are indeed a very strong-looking guardsman," Mira purred. "So your sister said. I was sure she must be exaggerating, but it seems she understated. Well, sisters. I suppose she is accustomed to the fine view. What's your name?"

"A—Ado," Adelis improvised. His eyes, in the shade of his brim, had grown quite wide, and his scored cheeks flushed.

Mira clapped her hands. "An Adriac name! Have you ever been there? It's a very fair, rich country, if one doesn't mind that touch of tertiary fever now and then." She favored him with a limpid moue. "You should pay it a visit."

Adelis gave Mira a third look, and a fourth. Nikys could see exactly when the coin dropped, because he yanked off his hat and threw it to the floor. "That," he said, in an entirely different voice, "is horrifying."

"How rude!" Mira sat up, fluttering her hand before her pouting lips. Penric turned his head to Nikys and added in his normal voice, "You know, I think we could really use a fan. Mira knows an entire sign language with them, very nuanced, although it may be out of date. Or Adriac in dialect. There's a translation project for me. I wonder if Zihre has one she would lend, somewhere in those miracle boxes of hers?"

"I imagine she would, and I'll bet you could make her laugh with it," said Nikys. She sat down on the bed beside him. Her. Them, howsoever. She turned to Adelis. "He fooled you for five minutes. Do you think he could fool a troop of border guards for a quarter-hour?"

"Unless they've taken to stripping travelers to the skin, yes." He added after a moment, "And maybe even then. If all he needs is to be not-Learned-Penric, Temple sorcerer." And after another, "I never had any doubt that *he* could escape the country, one way or another. Maybe even he and you together. That...is not the core of the problem." His hand crept to his lurid scars.

Nikys leaned forward, intent. "I had an idea about that." She glanced aside at Penric. "Is Mira the sort of woman who would have the whimsy to dress her servants in matching liveries?"

"Oh, yes."

"Perhaps with matching masks?"

"...Huh."

"One masked servant draws attention to himself. *Two* such servants draw attention to, I don't know, Mira?"

"Mira lived for attention," Penric conceded. "Well, in her public life, at least. Privately too, really."

Not scholar Penric's style at all, Nikys suspected, but he had certainly proved he could rise to any challenge.

Adelis's gaze kept flicking back and forth between Nikys and Penric. Or perhaps Nikys and Mira. Penric caught his eye and flipped at the curling copper hair, smirking. Adelis's lips flattened, and he turned his face away. He was still a little flushed.

"Then I," said Nikys determinedly, "shall do some sewing, if I can get the materials."

"I can help," offered Penric. "Cloth or skin, I make very tidy stitches."

She smiled up at him. *I'll bet you do.*

The part about *You are perfect as you are* she tucked away for later examination, like a child hoarding a sweet that she was afraid would be stolen by some stern grownup. *I have had to be my own grownup for a very long time now, haven't I?*

IV

---

*P*ENRIC WAS IMPRESSED with Nikys's forag-
ing abilities, as she gathered supplies for
their next project of disguise. They all retreated to
their room for the rest of the afternoon to carry
it out. Zihre had donated a pair of identical black
half-masks, broad across the upper face, modestly
ornamented with sequins. Nikys turned and cut up
a voluminous old black skirt for two tabards, which,
when she draped them over a black shirt and trousers for Adelis and a dark dress for herself, blended
well and gave them both a unified air. Done with
being fitted, and having run out of sandals to clean
and swords to sharpen, Adelis sat and watched.

"These should have matching embroidery and
more decoration," Nikys murmured, her borrowed

needle flashing in and out, "but there isn't time. This bit of braid around the edges must do."

"Everyday garb, perhaps," Penric offered, his fingers trying to equal her pace on the other piece. "I'm sure Mira provided her servants something showier for those exotic evenings, sadly delayed with the rest of her things by the accursed carters."

Nikys smiled into her work. Penric watched her covertly. Bent over in her concentration, she seemed utterly unaware of how enchanting she looked. Surely she was built to be the serene, solid center of...something. *My life,* he tried not to think. Because she would be stopping in Orbas with her brother, and he would be sailing back to Adria, right? He kept his needle moving.

But he couldn't stop picking at the impasse. *Like a scab?* "I know what Adelis plans when we get to Vilnoc," Penric said. "What of you?"

Nikys glanced up in surprise. "What?"

"Have you taken no thought for yourself?"

"While I have," Adelis put in, "Nikys will not lack."

Penric reflected, but refrained from observing aloud, that what Adelis had right now were the possessions they carried and a murderous pursuit. Both of which he was sharing equally with his sister, to be sure.

"Well, then," Pen tried again, "what would you desire? I mean, if you had a choice."

It was a little painful watching Nikys trying to wrap her imagination around the idea of having a *choice*. Or failing to. "What's the point of such speculation?" she asked in turn. "I'll deal with what chance drops in my way when it arrives there." The gesture she made put Pen uncomfortably in mind of a mourner throwing the first handful of dirt into a grave. Three times, he supposed, she had suffered her life to be upended by disaster overtaking those she'd depended upon: her father's sudden death, her husband's lingering one, and now Adelis's flight for his life. She glanced at her half-twin and away, but her needle didn't falter. "I did love the villa in Patos. I used to pretend it was mine. Just as well it wasn't, now."

She wants her own house? Pen tried to interpret this.

Most women do, Des returned, *at some point in their lives. Getting one without going through some man is made nearly impossible on purpose, I suspect.*

So would two small rooms in someone else's mansion overlooking a canal qualify? Sufficient for himself, they suddenly seemed a scanty offering.

"We won't be this poor for long," Adelis vowed. Less optimism, Pen suspected, than an effort to keep up his sister's morale. Adelis, too, had lost hugely in the late—ongoing—calamity, almost including his eyesight. Did that last recovery put the rest into an altered perspective?

Nikys shrugged. "Safety has nothing to do with being rich or poor. Or good or bad. A person could be as pious as you please, and own a palace, and still lose it all in a moment when the earth shakes its shoulders, or fire erupts." She frowned at her stitches. "Maybe true safety lies not in roots, but in feet. Or wings." She glanced, strangely, at Penric.

Bower birds, Pen thought. Didn't that breed try to attract females by producing elaborate, decorated nests?

Or there's that bird that hangs upside down from a branch by its toes, shakes its wings wildly, and screams for hours, Des put in with a spurious air of helpfulness. *You could try that.*

I'm not that desperate. Yet. Though even a rented villa seemed beyond his purse as a Temple divine.

Not beyond your ingenuity as a sorcerer, if you didn't continually underprice *our services.*

Our powers are a gift from the god. It seems wrong to hoard their benefits.

So put up your sign as a physician.

Penric's amusement congealed. *No.*

After a daunted pause, Des muttered, *Sorry. Not a good jest?*

No. Pen drew a steadying breath. *Never mind.*

He came to the end of his length of braid and tied off his thread, automatically using the one-handed technique a surgeon had taught him. Brows rising, Nikys paused to stare, then shook her head and kept sewing.

So what would I *desire, if I had a choice?* Pen thought to ask himself. One answer was obvious, and sat in front of him. But was the choice his to make?

You have many choices, Desdemona opined. *The real question is, what would you trade for them?*

෴

CONSULTING WITH Madame Zihre during her drainage treatment, Penric struck a bargain to earn another night's lodging and meals, not to mention their clothing and masks, by taking a seat that evening above the entry atrium and discreetly delousing any incoming clients in need of it. This proved to be a good third of them. In the persona of Sora Mira's own servant, neat in her black tabard and mask, Nikys attended upon him as they sheltered in a spot normally occupied by the upstairs maid. Penric wasn't sure which of them was guarding the other from any untoward notice, but in the event Zihre's customers seemed reasonably inhibited. If excessively inhabited.

It was all downhill magic, and so not costly, but really, such small prey made barely a nibble for Desdemona, given the demands of his own self-healing, still proceeding, and his work on Madame Zihre's tumor. He wondered if he might change clothes later and take to the rooftops in search of some better chaos sinks; and then there was the temple still to mulct. Zihre's house was proving a seductively comfortable respite, but they dared not linger long.

Toward midevening the influx of customers slacked off, and Penric decided he could leave his post and visit the garden, where Zihre provided food and drinks for her clients, as well as music and conversation. It simulated an impromptu, cresset-lit salon under the stars, although Penric expected the personalities and politics of this provincial town were nothing so rarified as in the aristocratic soirées of Lodi that Mira had once dominated.

They weren't half as rarified as they liked to pretend, Mira told him, amused.

In any case, it seemed a safe place to practice Mira a bit, before having to flaunt her at the potentially lethal audience of a border guard-post. Plus, he was getting peckish.

Trailed by Nikys, he shortened his stride to something more dainty as he navigated the stairs, managing not to wobble atop the clogs. *Do you have any idea*, sighed Mira, *what I could have done back then given your splendid inches?* Some dozen men and half-a-dozen women occupied the garden; he was a little startled when *all* their heads turned upon his entry. Not a few jaws hung open for a long moment, before their owners recovered them. He smiled benignly and selected a seat, a padded bench beneath a lantern hung on a post. *Good choice*, murmured Mira. *The light will really bring out our hair.*

Self-consciously, he leaned back and fluffed it a trifle, and wound a curl around his fingers. Nikys, bless her, guided a servant with a tray to him, and he selected a couple of snacks, aromatic meat wrapped in cooked grape leaves, and some bites of white cheese.

"Aren't you hungry?" he murmured to her.

"Servant, remember?" she whispered back. "I'd be dismissed for helping myself in front of guests."

"Mira, happily, is eccentric." He tapped her chin sternly and popped a grape-leaf-wrap into her mouth with his own slim fingers, and she smiled back unwilled. Possibly not such a wise move; abruptly, not all the men who were staring were staring only at him.

Three fellows circled in upon him, one abandoning his own partner to do so, to her dismay. The two younger ones were glowered off by the older, a broad, stocky man sporting a military haircut tipped with gray. The man had a face to launch a powerful glower, a trebuchet of a visage. Big, hooked nose, big chin, big ears; dark skin peppered with old smallpox scars; it reminded Pen of nothing so much as a well-worn boot, probably with hobnails. Yet it was redeemed from its remarkable ugliness by a pair of shrewd brown eyes, and more so by his slightly grim smile as he slid in beside Penric on the bench. Interestingly, he was not one of the visitors Penric had needed to secretly delouse, earlier. Nikys took up a maidservantly guard position behind them.

He captured Mira's hand. "Hello, there. You're new, are you?"

Penric allowed him to touch his lips to Mira's knuckles, and decided not to attempt a simper. "And you, I gather, are not?"

He chuckled. "Nothing new about me by now, no. Name's Chadro. And yours, lady?"

"You may call me Mira. Alas, I am not new either. I'm merely a guest of Madame Zihre's, breaking my journey here."

His heavy eyebrows went up in disappointment. "Not an employee of the house, then, Mira?"

Pen shook his head.

"Ah. Pity." He set Pen's hand down upon his skirted thigh, and patted it. "How do you know Zihre?"

"We'd not met before yesterday, but we share a mutual friend, in whose name I was able to presume upon her gracious hospitality."

"Do you..." He hesitated. "Might this friend, and you, by chance also share Zihre's trade?"

"I used to, but I am retiring to, shall we call it, private service. Hence the journey."

"Really." His smile crept back. So did his hand. "But not retired yet?"

"You tempt me, sir, but I have these pending obligations."

"You lie very nicely. Kind Mira. I can't imagine this face tempts you much."

"One part is not the whole of a man, nor the whole measure of a man's worth."

"Hah." His amusement grew. "You make a prettier philosopher than most I've met."

Mira smiled. "Not a high bar to leap over, I daresay."

"Indeed, not. If you—" But his next foray into this faintly ponderous banter was interrupted by an altercation from the atrium, which spilled violently into the garden.

Two red-faced young men, both with poniards drawn, circled each other, seeking space. The other occupants of the garden gave it to them, scattering back to the walls with alarmed cries. The young men were both well-dressed in the local style, with elaborated hair that suggested neither were of the military persuasion that so many of the clients here shared. A couple of servants dropped their trays and raced out, calling for help from the porter and Zihre.

"Berat scum!" one cried. "A pox upon your house, and you!"

"Parga dog! I'll cut out your lying tongue!"

They barged forward, meeting in a shrill scrape of steel.

"Oh, gods," groaned Chadro. "Who let those idiots in here both at the same time?" Unlike every other more prudent witness, when he rose he stepped not back but forward.

Penric matched him. The last thing his party needed was for a brawl to turn bloody, bringing in the local authorities to question and closely examine everyone present, including the passing travelers. As strangers, they'd draw attention, and with enough attention someone might well put together the manservant with the burn scars on his face, and whatever circular from the capital for Adelis's arrest that had arrived by now. This had to be stopped, and Penric had the means. To manage it discreetly, not revealing his powers, was going to be trickier...

Des, speed me. As slippery as a snake, Penric weaved between the two opponents, managing to grab one knife-clutching hand by the wrist. He dodged a flash from behind, though it clipped a curl from his hair. A quick twist to the nerve beneath the skin, and the hand flew open, dropping the poniard. He swung his leg around behind his victim's knees, disguising a jab to the nerves there and dropping the fellow neatly to the ground. Chadro meanwhile had stepped behind the other man and slid his muscular arms through his armpits, lifting him off his feet with a jerk and trapping him close. One strong shake, like a dog dispatching a rat, and the second poniard followed the first to the paving stones, clattering.

"That's enough!" barked Chadro, his voice deep and loud; parade-ground pitched, charged with authority. "I'll cool both your hot heads upside down in the well if you don't settle!" Penric didn't doubt Chadro could and would do it, too, and apparently no one else doubted it either.

Penric bent and quickly collected both poniards, and another knife concealed beneath his man's jacket at the small of his back, and yet another hidden in the other's boot. Clutching the cutlery, he danced back out of range of it all, smiling and catching his breath. A couple of the young men with military haircuts belatedly stepped forward to aid Chadro, taking his prisoner off his hands, and the big porter arrived at last, looking both alarmed and irate. Penric's man wasn't exactly standing up yet, crouched over clutching his paralyzed right hand with his left, though he would recover the use of his no-doubt-tingling limbs in a few minutes. Probably.

Chadro bent and scooped up something off the pavement, and lumbered to Pen's side. "Lady," he said earnestly, "you should not have run between those two wild men. They nearly knifed you." He held out his hand, in which lay the shining copper scrap of Pen's hair.

About to protest *I was perfectly safe,* Pen was interrupted by the portion of Desdemona that was Mira. *Leave this to me, oh-so-Learned, or you will botch it.* Bemused, he let Mira take over. "Oh, my!" she gasped, as Chadro captured her hand and tipped the curl into her palm. "I never saw. So good that you stopped him."

"Whatever possessed you, to attempt that?"

A true explanation of what possessed Penric would take all night, he thought wryly. "I was thinking only that Madame Zihre did not deserve the disruption to her household."

"Very true." He frowned up at her. "What did you do to the one that you put down? You were very quick."

"Oh"—Mira flipped at her hair—"I was taught a few tricks, early in my trade, for discouraging obstreperous clients." She took Chadro's thick paw and pressed the curl into it. "You may as well keep it. I can't put it back."

His hand closed around it, and he smiled. "I suppose not."

Penric looked around for Nikys, who had sensibly, thank their mutual god, hung back behind the bench. Her dark eyes wide with fear, she hurried forward to his side, gripping his arm tight. He could feel her hand shake. "Sora Mira! Are you all right?" She did not add, *You cursed fool!* but he thought he detected it in the set of her jaw.

"Perfectly all right, thanks to this gentleman here," Mira purred, and Nikys shot her—him—them—an even more scorching look, quickly concealed as she bent her face. She swallowed and regained control of her features, or at least, her distressed gaze was sufficiently in-character for a lady's loyal maidservant.

Madame Zihre appeared, looking rather rumpled, to sort out the contretemps, and Pen faded back a little more. The clash had started when the two young men had both attempted to choose the same lady for the evening, apparently for no better reason than to thwart the other. With the air of a mother sending unruly children to bed without their suppers, Zihre decreed that neither should have the girl, instead assigning them two others, or they could take themselves back out to the street with no refunds.

"My knives!" protested one, unwisely. Indeed, giving them back their weapons even upon their departure invited them to take up their brawl again as soon as they got outside.

"Madame Zihre," said Penric, "might I suggest a servant be dispatched to deliver their weapons to their respective parents, together with an explanation as to why. They can each beg their property back from their fathers in the morning."

Both paled, the one standing shooting Pen a look of extreme dislike, the one still seated a look of dislike mixed with dread. Chadro grinned. Zihre nodded dry agreement, and consigned the blades to a manservant to so dispose of. The angry, but cowed, rivals were drawn up opposite stairs by their girls, whom Penric suspected Zihre had selected more for reliable sense than looks.

"I trust those two will be delivered out the front door, later, at different times," he murmured to her.

"Oh, yes," she agreed distractedly. "Thank you for your aid, Ler—Sora Mira." She turned and added, "And you, General Chadro. Without your quick wits and work, that could have been the most dreadful mess."

Penric blinked. *Well, that explains some things…* At that rank, and clearly active duty, Chadro could only be the commander of the whatever-number-it-was Imperial infantry that Adelis had identified as the local garrison. Fourteenth, that was it. Ye gods, did he and Adelis know each other?

She continued to Chadro, "Consider your entertainment on the house tonight, sir."

"Hm," he said, "about that…" He sent Mira a faint smile and drew Zihre into the atrium. Penric pricked his ears, but could not quite make out their low-voiced consultation, except that they took turns glancing back into the garden. Zihre made some rather helpless palms-out gestures, and shrugged. Chadro grimaced unhappily. After another minute of even lower-voiced exchange, they returned, Zihre looking apologetic, Chadro frustrated.

Chadro seated himself again beside Mira, converting his frown to a wry smile. "Zihre tells me you are your own woman, and if I wish to seduce you, I will have to do so without her aid."

"Well, that's true. Mine was a hard-won autonomy, and I do not hold it lightly."

"Rather cruel, from my point of view. Throwing me back on my meager resources. If I had any kind of skill with women, Zihre would not find me near so profitable a client."

"Take heart, sir. I doubt there is any man in Sosie who could afford me."

Chadro cast Mira an oddly shy sidewise glance. "I could try."

She smiled back, and stroked him kindly on the cheek. Interrupting this exchange, Penric leaned down to Chadro's ear and whispered conspiratorially behind his hand, "It's no use in any case. It's that time of month when I am compelled to take a few days off." There, that should settle things without hard feelings. He was just sitting back, satisfied, when Mira added, "Although I have a number of pleasant ways around such issues. A man would have to be willing to place himself entirely in my hands, however."

Mira...!

"I can think of no fate more delightful," murmured Chadro, "than to place myself entirely in your hands, Sora Mira." He followed this up with another brush of his lips upon Mira's knuckles, and Penric began to think Chadro's humble self-presentation was as sham as his own. Granted, a man with his looks had strong motivation to perfect charm.

"If you truly mean that," said Mira, "you might provide me with as much amusement as I provide you. Making up any shortfall in our arrangement."

"Oh," breathed Chadro, "I truly do."

"Then negotiate with Madame Zihre for the use of her room, and I will show you secrets of Lodi that have made slaves of dukes."

Chadro rose with alacrity, and made his way over to Zihre, who was quietly dealing with a servant by the kitchen door.

Mira, what are you about? asked Penric in panic. *Are you out of my mind?*

Come, come, Penric, and now she sounded rather like Ruchia, brisk and practical while proposing lunacy. *We have sat through any number of your bedroom ventures over the years. Turnabout is fair play.* She added after a moment, *Also, you will learn some new things. That should appeal to the scholar in you.*

We can't let ourselves be trapped in a room with him!

On the contrary, I plan to trap him in a room with me. I had his measure in the first five minutes, Penric. Trust me. You will never take your clothes off, he will be very happy, and that little problem of financing the next leg of our journey will be solved.

Pointing out that he planned to rob the temple felt like a weak counter-argument, given that there was no certainty the Sosie temple would yield anything. Also, it did not quite seem the moral high ground.

Nikys leaned over his shoulder to whisper in alarm, "Penric, what are you *doing*?"

"Mira has some idea," he whispered back. Mira, in Pen's prior experience, had many ideas, some of them scandalous. "She *is* the expert here…"

Briefly, he considered trying for some consensus, or veto, from all ten of the personalities that made up his chaos demon, but in bedroom matters that tended to be more of a cacophony. Learned Ruchia would vote with Mira, and so would Vasia of Patos. The two physicians, Amberein and Helvia, would just laugh at him. Learned Aulia of Brajar would sit it out, feigning dignity, although he gathered she was entertained by the results regardless. Umelan the Roknari hated men generally, not without cause. Rogaska had no use for anyone. The Cedonians Litikone and Sugane, Desdemona's first human riders, tended to blur together after two hundred years, although he suspected Sugane had liked women. *So do I, blast it.* The lioness and the mare, thankfully, never offered comment; Pen supposed, as creatures subject to heats, they'd never had to deal with such human complications. He was beginning to envy them.

Chadro returned with Zihre, gone wide-eyed, in tow. "Sora Mira," she said hesitantly, "are you certain? I assure you, my hospitality does not depend on you doing anything you...you do not care to do."

Mira favored her with Penric's sunniest grin. She stepped back, her hand going to her throat, and Chadro, watching anxiously, vented a faint *Oh* like a man hit in the stomach. "I promise you," said Mira, and Penric imagined that *you* was inclusive, "everything will be all right."

Zihre raised her hands in a feeble gesture of *upon your head be it*, and led them upstairs. Nikys crowded close behind. As Zihre opened the door to her bedroom, Mira inquired lightly, "Zihre, do you chance to have a supply of silk scarves or the like? Preferably the like; silk *knots* so."

"No chance to it. Top layer of that green chest, together with, ah, some other things. Which may be better to the purpose."

"Excellent." Mira swept inside with the air of a queen reclaiming her country. Chadro followed in hopeful curiosity, like the queen's loyal general sworn to her service.

Mira, this is madness, Pen complained, by now half-terrified. Most of the other half of him appeared to be gathering to watch events unfold like spectators to an archery match.

Not at all, said Mira serenely. *Back in the later days of my career in Lodi, I made something of a specialty of elderly gentlemen. They dubbed me the Resurrection Woman. I had expected my income to fall with age, but in fact it rose. Very satisfying.*

Chadro isn't elderly!

So much the better. Mira smirked.

He could probably break me in half with his bare hands. If he figures out who I really am, he'll kill me!

If he figures out what any of us really are, he'll likely kill us all. Compelled to by his orders, if nothing else. This adds nothing to our risk.

Gods, that reeked of a Ruchia-argument, twisty as a braid and as fitted to hang him. He'd often wondered if that was an effect of her scholarly Temple training, but really, it was probably just Ruchia. Was this a foretaste of his demon ascending?

You could take back control at any time, and that was clearly Des altogether, *but I advise against it. After all, you wouldn't jog the elbow of an expert acrobat juggling fire.*

"Sora Mira," the dismayed Nikys choked, "I will remain right outside your door. Call me if you need *anything at all.*" Rescue being strongly implied.

Bad plan, opined Mira. *I don't know yet how noisy a man Chadro is. Too much room for mistakes. And I know you like her, but do you really think she could interrupt subtly enough?*

Pen had no idea, besides wanting to keep Nikys as far apart from this misadventure as possible. Like, in another country. Which, in fact, was the end goal. He must not lose sight of that. If events turned to disaster in Mira's hands, he could probably rescue himself despite Chadro's unnerving burliness, although betraying the secret of his sorcerer's status, but... "No," Pen said, "go join your brother in our room. Stay there." He wasn't sure how to convey *Get ready to run,* but Chadro was already closing the door upon their two wildly anxious escorts.

Chadro twisted the key in the lock and turned to Mira, smiling wryly. "Sora Mira, I do believe your maidservant is in love with you. I cannot fault her for it."

Penric coughed. "Surely not." Or at any rate, not for much longer.

"She was certainly looking daggers at me. Ready to bite. Clearly, I had better return you without a hair out of place."

Desdemona inquired, half-sweet, half-serious, *If Nikys were not watching, dear Pen, would you even care? Or would you find this just one more odd adventure with us?*

Pen could only manage a sort of mental mumble.

Because if Nikys is going to take up with you, she is perforce going to take up with all of us. Or do you somehow imagine you can, across years, hide from your most intimate companion everything you really are?

Are, had become, was still becoming...

Because that never ends well.

Two hundred years of experience speaking, across ten very different lives? Twelve, counting the lioness and the mare. Penric went silent in temporary surrender, letting Mira go hunt up her supplies.

V

NIKYS RETURNED RELUCTANTLY to their room. Adelis, last left dozing on his pallet, was up and pacing from wall to wall. He'd had the least to do, hiding all day in here, and the forced delay in their flight was making him tenser and tenser.

"Finally!" he said to her. "What's happening out there? Where's Penric? Is he still flouncing around in that bloody dress?"

"I have no idea what he thinks he's doing. Adelis, did you ever know a General Chadro?"

Adelis halted. "Egin Chadro?"

"I didn't catch his given name. He apparently commands the Fourteenth, here in Sosie."

"He's out there? In this house?"

"Yes. Is he someone who would recognize you?"

"Yes, very likely."

"How well do you know him?"

"We served together a few years ago. Very level-headed officer, but lacking a rich or well-connected family to foster his career. If he's been promoted to the Fourteenth, someone is finally doing something right."

"Does he have a short temper?'

"He doesn't suffer fools gladly. Or at all. Why do you ask?"

"He was very taken with Mira."

Adelis grumbled something unintelligible. And grudgingly granted, "Penric was very convincing."

"And I think Mira was very taken with him. She's taken him off to Zihre's bedchamber, anyway. I can't imagine what she's up to in there with him." Rather, Nikys could *imagine* quite a lot, but most of it ended in bloodshed.

"Is he *insane?*" Adelis sputtered, and Nikys had no doubt which *he* was meant.

She contemplated the question. By the standards of anyone not a Temple sorcerer, was Penric mad? Or should she only be asking if he was mad *by* the standards of sorcerers? She was beginning to wonder about sorcerers in ways that had never crossed her mind when they were just a distant rumor or a rare glimpse of white robes.

"I don't suppose General Chadro likes lads?" she tried, in a weak sort of hopefulness. "Do you know?"

"Not that I'd ever heard. I can guarantee he wouldn't like being made a game of."

"Oh."

Adelis eyed her. "I think we had better pack up. We may have to run."

She nodded shortly, feeling sick. "How long should we give it?"

"No idea. Although Chadro does not suffer fools quietly, either. If there's an uproar, we'll hear it."

"All the way across the house?" Zihre's bed-chamber was in the far corner of the inner atrium.

"Maybe. Bastard's teeth grind us all." And never had the oath seemed more apt. "If Penric's unmasked and arrested, we'll have to leave him to get himself out."

He's never abandoned us. Not once. The cry teetered on a see-saw with *What does that long lunatic expect to happen?* trapping Nikys voiceless between her offense and her dread.

They fell into a quick collaboration, bundling their possessions into two parcels. Nikys stacked Penric's scant clothing ready on the bed. Penric's medical case she set apart, though she made sure it was all neatly packed. Adelis kept his sword out. It didn't take long, and then they had little to do but sit side-by-side on the bed and listen to the occasional voices or footsteps crossing the gallery, more muted and infrequent as the night grew old. Nikys rose and pushed the door ajar, tilting her head intently, but heard nothing more than a household settling down. Adelis finally stretched himself on his pallet, fully dressed with his sword by his hand, and dozed, so Nikys forbore pacing. She jittered in place, instead, flexing her feet and knees.

It must have been two hours before she heard footfalls approaching on the gallery—barefoot padding, not the clunk of clogs. And since when could she recognize those steps unseen? She jumped up. The door swung open, and Penric appeared, still entirely Mira from copper-gilt top to lacquered toe, although he held the clogs in one hand. His dress did not seem disarrayed. No blood. He shut the door and leaned against it with a tired whoosh of breath. His eyes were dark and a bit wild, reminding her for some reason of a clumsy cat they had once fished out of a cistern.

"Well," he said, his voice dropping from Mira's through its normal register to something that also could have come out of the cistern. "That was an experience."

Adelis was on his feet. "Where's Chadro?"

"I left him sleeping like the dead. I'm not sure if Zihre will let him occupy her bed till morning, or wake him up and toss him out."

"What did you *do* to him?" asked Nikys. "Something magic?" Magic, illusion...surely Penric if anyone could manage something like that. Maybe he hadn't had to do anything...real. She glanced at Adelis's half-healed scars, and his wholly healed eyes. *But sorcery is real.*

Penric was silent for a long moment. He finally said, "Mira does not gossip about her clients. Very rigid rule, I gather. The highest rank of Lodi courtesans don't; that's part of how they become the highest rank."

Adelis was giving him a very sideways look, his lips flat, but he did not choose to press for details. At least not in front of Nikys. It was maddening.

She said urgently, "You weren't hurt? You took no...no insult?"

"Not at all." Penric grimaced and spread his fingers. "It's all right, Nikys. I kept my clothes on, and I didn't have my hands anywhere they'd not been as a physician. Better, actually, since this body was still alive. There were good reasons we taught anatomy in the winter. And I washed them before and after, all the same."

Since, as an anatomist, he'd taken bodies *entirely apart*, Nikys did not find this in the least reassuring. And how well was she growing to know him, that she could spot his misdirections so readily?

"More importantly," Adelis cut in, "do you think Chadro saw through your disguise?"

Penric seemed to consider this question seriously, then replied, quite simply, "No." He thumped his head back against the door, stretching his neck and rolling his shoulders. "Ah, gods, I'm tired. Well, no help for it. Nikys, aid me getting out of Mira and back into my own clothes. Carefully; we're still going to need her in the morning."

He took two steps forward, stopped, and slapped his hands against his torso in dismay. "Oh, *shit!*"

Since Penric had to be the least foul-mouthed man she'd ever met, Nikys found this oath quite startling. She gasped, "What's the matter?"

"I forgot to ask for money. *Mira* forgot, if you can believe it. I thought she seemed overexcited. All that for...shit, *shit*." He took a deep, recovering breath. "Well. It may be possible to get into the Sosie temple now. And oh my dear bleached god, I need to dump some disorder on the way. It's been building up in me all day. Like water behind a dam. Tiny insects are useless for this much chaos, and besides, there aren't any left around here."

If he noticed their possessions packed for flight, he made no remark on it. Perforce, she helped him out of his Mira-togs, laying them aside. Nikys had never believed that clothes made the man, but the lack of them certainly did; it was weirdly heartening to see the familiar Penric emerge again from the disguise...and, perhaps, from the domination of his demon? Because she was increasingly convinced that Mira had been something more than skin-deep. More than an act.

So...so Penric had evidently done some things tonight that would horrify her to have to do. Men did. Shoved swords into people, for example, or sacked towns. But she found herself drawing away from him despite the arguments of common sense. Would she be happier with him if he'd seemed more distraught? That at least would be a reaction she could understand.

Instead, she asked, "How will you get out of the house unseen?"

"There's a tradesman's door in the back wall by the laundry. I don't need a lantern, so slipping out in the dark should be easy."

And if it's locked? she started to ask, then realized it was a foolish remark. She'd seen what he could do to locks. There were barriers that could thwart sorcerers, evidently, but ordinary locks weren't one of them.

And then he was gone, flitting out as silently as a cat. But this time, she thought of those big wild-cats in the northern mountains, the ones that took lambs and kids in the night. She'd long been aware that Penric was a strange man, but she'd somehow thought him *safe*.

What, as Adelis, or Kymis, or Chadro were safe? For all of Penric's soft-voiced self-effacement, the ignore-me-I'm-harmless smiles, she was beginning to realize he might be the least safe man she'd ever met. Or, certainly, the least predictable...perhaps that was the root of it. Most men kept to their assigned parts in life. If you knew the part, you could reliably guess how they would behave. She had no script for *demon-ridden sorcerer*.

And nor did Adelis, she supposed. Penric had powers Adelis could neither see nor counter by any military skill. She wondered if Pen realized her brother's stiffness toward him had its roots in well-stifled fear. Or if Adelis did, for that matter.

The next hour of fretting was a reprise of the first two, although her exhaustion was such that she lay down in her pallet beside Adelis's. He slept; she couldn't. At last, Penric ghosted back in, not heralded by any night-candle. The one on the wash-stand that barely kept the room from total darkness was guttering.

Adelis sat up with Nikys. "Any trouble?" he asked.

Penric waved a hand in the dimness. "Yes and no. I wasn't seen. But the Sosie temple evidently clears its offering boxes when they lock up at night. Not a single coin to be found."

Adelis frowned. "There might have been objects of value. Good candlesticks, plate..."

"Yes, and all of it too recognizable to try to pawn in this town." Penric's voice took an unaccustomed edge. "Since the whole point of the exercise is to get out of this town, not a useful thought. Which I already had, believe me." He paused only to strip himself of his jacket and trousers, and flop into the bed in his shirt and trews. "Ah, gods." He added after a moment, "I did manage to divest all today's chaos. There was a sick street dog. Poor beast."

Taking this in, Nikys discovered a new curiosity. "How did you rid yourself of all that chaos back when you were working for the Mother's Order in Martensbridge?"

A faint snort from the bed. "I struck a bargain with a Martensbridge butcher. I'd once treated his daughter. He let me do his slaughtering. It bore a double benefit; I was able to unload an enormous amount of disorder on a regular schedule, and the animals died painlessly, without fear or distress. It seemed to be theologically allowable, or at least no god chided me. Thankfully. My superiors were delighted with the scheme. It allowed them to use me to my uttermost limits."

And beyond, until he'd broken, as Nikys understood another night-confession, back in the temple in Skirose. Which Adelis had not witnessed, and

she had not relayed, she was reminded. She was not moved to explain it to him now.

"It worked well," Penric's reminiscence went on. "Although I stopped eating meat for a while. Odd. I never had that trouble with animals we hunted, or butchered on the farm." His head fell back on his pillow, and he signed himself. His voice seemed to come more from underneath the bed than atop it. "Tomorrow, we need a new plan. This one is growing overcomplicated."

"You think so?" growled Adelis, sardonic.

Penric did not attempt a reply.

THE NEXT morning, when they were all still sodden with sleep after the late night, they were awakened by a knock at their door. Nikys dragged herself from her pallet and went to answer it, drawing her role as maidservant around her like a rumpled robe. But it was Madame Zihre, alone. Nikys let her in and closed the door firmly in her wake, as Penric, sitting up blearily in the bed, was still very much Penric, flat-chested and stubble-chinned.

Zihre strode to the bedside and planted her fists on her hips, staring at him. "*What* did you do to poor General Chadro last night, *Learned?*"

Penric rubbed his face, and visibly choked back a first defensive protest of *Nothing!* as plainly untrue. "Why do you ask? Did he have a complaint?" He went still, swallowing. "Did he realize what I really was?"

"I have no idea what you really are," said Zihre, sounding exasperated. "But no, he had no complaints. He did send this, by special messenger just now." She thrust out a small coin-bag.

"Oh!" said Penric, surprised. "An honest man, five gods pour blessings upon his boot-faced head!" He took it, fingers jingling the contents through the cloth. "If this is silver, and not copper, which would be a bit of an insult, we may be able to hire a coach to continue our journey after all." He straightened the counterpane across his lap for a tray, and upended the bag upon it. Zihre, Nikys, and Adelis with his hat pulled down again, though it was futile for disguise at this range, all crowded around the bed to see.

A chiming stream of metal the real color of Penric's hair poured out into a little pile.

Everyone fell silent for a long moment, staring at the glowing gold.

"That," said Nikys, shaken, "could *buy* us a coach."

"And a team," added Adelis. "Matched."

"Well," Penric took a breath, "that was certainly the style in which Mira always traveled."

Nikys gulped for her scattering wits. "Except that would be wasteful."

Penric's lips twitched back in a swift, short grin, though she wasn't sure how she'd amused him.

LEARNED PENRIC pointedly declined to entrust the new purse to Adelis, or to Nikys who might yield it to Adelis—Adelis's cheeks darkened slightly at the reminder of his duplicity against Penric back at Skirose, before they'd fled over the hills. So by the time they had broken their fast, and done Penric up again as Mira, and he and Nikys, prudently escorted by a manservant borrowed from Zihre, made their way to a livery to arrange matters, it was nearly noon before they left the gates of Sosie in the hired coach. The postilion swung his team east down the river road at a smart trot.

Penric had delayed their departure yet more by going aside with Zihre for a change of her compress and one last treatment of her tumor. Trying not to admit anything, he'd talked all around cautioning her to say nothing of what she'd really learned of her guests. But Nikys thought the woman received the warning well enough. Her good-byes were ambiguous, though polite. Although she did remark that if Learned Jurald ever found himself interdicted by the Temple, she might find work for him in her house. At least she didn't ask for restoration of her loaned garments.

As the road curved, Nikys looked back at the town on its height. "Do you think you will ever return there in the future, Penric? To see if what you tried to do for Madame Zihre succeeded?"

Penric leaned his head against the worn leather squabs of the seatback, and closed his eyes. "No," he said.

Despite the dress, the hair, the makeup, he did not look very Mira in this moment, and Nikys wondered at the difference, and then at herself for finding it so readily discernible. She hesitated. "Why not?"

"If it worked, I don't need to know, and if it didn't, I don't want to know." He turned aside, pretending to doze. The pose was not persuasive.

Adelis, fingers drumming on his knees, stared out at the river. Sosie guarded the dwindling head of navigation for the stream, the craft that could reach it more skiffs than barges. "We should have caught or stolen one of those boats, day before yesterday," he mused. "Or offered to work our passage like the grain wagon. We'd be nearly to the coast by now."

With none of the appalling risks their recent sojourn had occasioned, it went unsaid. Eyes still closed, Penric grimaced. It might be true. It also, Nikys thought, neatly undercut all that Penric had done for them in the past two days, pushing himself to his peculiar limits.

Five gods, I cannot wait for this journey to be over.

VI

THEIR COACH WAS three-fourths of the way to the border when darkness overtook them. After some debate, Penric ruled that they should stop at the next coaching inn to eat and sleep, rather than paying extra for night service. Mira would be rumpled and unattractive at the border post if they rode all night, such travel was rare and thus more likely to draw suspicion, and Adelis would do better to present his petition for refuge at the court of Orbas in daylight. Adelis was on edge at the delay. Penric couldn't blame him.

The inn proved modest and clean, but Mira was sulking, and left Pen to play her part by himself. Fortunately, it was brief, the traveling courtesan's gold coins speaking for her, speeding the negotiation for a private chamber and dinner to be brought up. Desdemona as a whole was still talking to him, though she didn't seem to have much to say.

Nikys was scarcely talking to him either, plainly repelled by his last night's—surprisingly successful—ploy. Really Mira's ploy, but what was the point of him protesting? It would just make it sound as if his demon was in imminent danger of ascending, hardly an improvement. It must be enough just to get Nikys and her brother over the frontier safely, which, after all, was the task he'd started out to complete. Anything else, including gratitude, would be a boon that he couldn't do anything about anyway, right? It was better that she was peeved with him. It would make parting less painful. Right?

The reflection that their whole detour to Sosie might well have been the Bastard's answer to prayers none of their own was too disturbing to dwell upon. As they blew out the candles and settled into their beds, Penric turned his mind to more practical matters.

Vilnoc would be his first chance to report in at his own Order since news of his execution-or-escape from the bottle dungeon in Patos. There had been time by now for first words of the fate of their envoy to get back to Lodi, to the duke and to Pen's archdivine, but Pen had no guess what stories they'd received, let alone believed. They might think him dead. Pen wondered morbidly if the archdivine would have claimed all his books, or yielded them to the duke, or broken them up for sale.

And if his treasured volumes were gone beyond recall, what did he have to go back for, really? He toyed with the notion of staying dead. It would be a very clever, tidy escape from all his oaths and disciplines, to be sure. Except that he didn't really want to. He'd no heart to abandon the reputation for learning that he'd spent the last ten years building, and a scholar needed a rich patron. It was not the sort of work ordinary men would understand or pay for, not seeing immediate benefit to themselves.

Keep it in mind for your future self, then, murmured Des, slyly, enduring his fretting. As if she had a choice to do otherwise than endure him, any more than he did her.

Des!

But his outrage was weak.

THEY MADE a reasonably early start the next morning, despite delays for making up Mira to her most polished perfection that had Adelis's hand clenching on his sword hilt with impatience. But at last, escorted by her matched pair of masked and tabarded servants, Mira swept aboard, and they were off again. Only twenty-five miles more. One more relay of horses would do it, although they would be compelled to exchange both horses and coach again at the border village, leaving their Cedonian transport behind and picking up men and beasts of Orbas. No doubt at a premium price, but at least that assured such services would be waiting. Skinning foreign travelers trapped by border laws was a happy tradition for such countrymen, in both directions.

They had made their first change, with but ten miles left to go, when Adelis, painfully tense, turned his head. "Hoofbeats. Horses. Galloping behind us."

"Put your mask back on before you stick your head out, sunder it," Pen demanded. Adelis glared but complied. Nikys gave him a glance for this rare black profanity, and took to the other window.

"Cavalrymen. Half a dozen of them," she reported.

Adelis swore. "Bastard's teeth and Mother's blood. It's Egin Chadro. Come for his revenge on you, Penric?"

"Can the coach outrun them to the border? If you offer the postilion gold?" asked Nikys.

"Not a chance," said Adelis. "Still too far. They're bound to overtake us in another mile. We'll have to fight." He readied his knife in his belt sheath, and set the sword beside him. Extracted the bow from the wrapped bundle, strung it, and retrieved their scant handful of arrows. Frowned at Penric. "We've taken down that many men before, between us. Can you do your magic tricks again, Penric? Pull the bow, or should I give it to Nikys? Or will you be afraid to muss your dress?"

Penric ignored the trailing insult. He wanted to think fast, but he mostly thought of his quiet study above the canal, suddenly missed. "It would only take one survivor to warn the border against us, and bring back a swarm of reinforcements. He wouldn't have far to ride."

Adelis's teeth set. "Then we had better make sure none get away, eh?"

Penric contemplated the potential chaos. Was this a gift of his god? *If so, I don't want it, Sir.* "It's a busy road. A single passing witness could get away and do the same. Or a coach-load. I don't think we can count on privacy for such a bloody brawl." He slid over beside Nikys and risked a glance himself. The horsemen were close enough now for a deep bellow to be faintly heard over their own team's hoofbeats and harness-jingle, and the creaking of the coach. "Wait."

"What?" said Adelis, outraged. "Have you lost your wits?" His mouth thinned. "Or are you betraying us at the last? What were you really talking about with Chadro all those hours night before last?"

"Not that," said Penric, fervently. "Listen."

The bellow became words: "Sora Mira! Stop! Please!"

"Don't you think," said Penric slowly, "that if he'd learned of my disguise, he would be yelling something more like *Stop so I can kill you, Jurald, you lying son-of-a-bitch?*"

Nikys's eyebrows climbed. "Would he?"

"...Unless he's being clever. Is he that clever, Adelis?"

"Maybe." Adelis's hand worked on his hilt. "Maybe."

"Because if he still believes I'm Mira, I think I could talk our way out of this." Whatever this was. "Give him his remaining gold back, something." *Right, Mira? Right?*

The return silence was palpable, and pointed.

Pen scrambled to persuade her. *Lovely Mira, if I was insufficiently admiring of all your hard work, I apologize, and I promise to make it up later—but only if there is a later. Besides, if we get slaughtered here on this road, where would you all jump? I mean, I know you liked Chadro, but surely not in that way?*

Desdemona-as-a-whole snorted. *An admirable man, but he does not have a swift and malleable mind. Not like you, young Penric.*

"We can still fight after we talk," Nikys gulped, "but we can't still talk after we fight. I think we'd better let Penric try first."

Adelis set his jaw on fulmination, but choked out, "Perhaps so."

Pen managed a short nod. "Stay in the coach, out of sight, Adelis. Those masks are enough to mislead anyone who hasn't met you, but not someone who has. If things go badly, I'll try to send a couple of horses your way. Or cut loose the leaders, or anything I can. Ride and don't look back."

"Don't try to explain my trade to me," growled Adelis, "and I'll not try to explain yours to you."

The grinning cavalrymen were riding up around them, one of them grabbing for the surprised postilion, another for the coach horses' checkreins. Their hoots for a halt sounded more cheery than murderous. The coach rumbled to a stop over the protests, but not the resistance, of the postilion. Chadro cantered up and swung his lathered horse to the door, blocking it. The animal's nostrils were round and red and blowing. Chadro was in scarcely better shape, though as exultant as a successful runner at the end of a god's-day race. His boot-face was damp with sweat as his chest rose and fell.

Pen signed himself, tapped his thumb five times against his lips, took a deep breath, fixed a smile in place, and leaned out the window.

"Dear Egin!" he cried, endeavoring to sound surprised. "What are you doing here?"

"I thought you'd still be resting at Zihre's place. I didn't expect you to leave so soon. I came last night to speak to you, but you were already gone."

"I do have, as I mentioned, an obligation, and we were already much delayed."

Chadro dismounted, handed off his reins to an attentive soldier, and looked up at her. "Mira, would you walk a little apart with me? What I have to say is for no one's ears but yours."

Pen's lips parted in doubt, but Mira spoke up at last: *Oh, for pity's sake. It's not like I haven't acted in this playlet before, too many times to remember. Stand aside, Learned Fool. I couldn't bear to watch you flounder.*

Relieved, Pen yielded the lead to her, though on guard to take it all back in an instant. She dismounted from the coach into Chadro's helping arms rather more gracefully than Pen could have managed. Her smile was grateful and soft. Chadro's grip was understandably hot, and Pen quickly captured his hands to keep them from straying anywhere near his underpadding. No convenient bedposts and bindings here, and his costume was only meant to fool the eye.

Mira hooked her elbow through Chadro's as they sauntered up the verge away from the straining ears and avidly curious eyes of both their escorts. An old plane tree stood near the road, and Chadro led her into its speckled shade, a few papery fallen leaves crackling underfoot, then turned to take both her hands in his. Pen looked down into his earnest, ugly features; he was a good half a head taller than the general even without the clogs. Chadro looked up like a man kneeling before an altar.

"What would it take to make you stay with me, Mira?"

"I cannot stay. I told you I was journeying, and why."

"Yes, you've been wholly honest with me..."

Ouch, ouch, ouch.

"Yet you plan to tarry for one man. Why not another?"

"My course has already been laid."

He ducked his chin. "I expect the lucky fellow only thinks to give you some private portion." He took a breath. "How if I outbid him? Marry me, and all I have will be yours."

"Oh, Egin," Mira sighed. "Do you think I haven't received such proposals before, from other great men?"

That's laying it on with a trowel, isn't it? thought Pen.

No, it's quite true. Mira tapped Chadro on his big hooked nose, in a friendly but distancing fashion. She continued to him, "When I get to Orbas, I must make a final choice of service between two dukes."

That, Pen realized, was also perfectly true. Although the duke of Adria had never shown any sign of wanting to bed him. Thankfully.

Chadro swallowed, taken aback. But not for long, because he was, clearly, not a man who surrendered readily, or he would not have achieved his present rank. "But I daresay neither offers you marriage."

"No. That is their attraction."

"You don't have to sail so isolate. I could be your harbor. Your rock."

"You're a soldier, Egin. You must serve at your emperor's pleasure, not mine. One unlucky moment in battle, and my rock turns to sand. Or grave dirt."

"A Cedonian general's widow is not without resources."

"Exchanging my wedding garlands for bier wreaths? I like you well, but I am not drawn to such a ceremony."

You know, this man really is terrible at courting women, Pen observed in bemusement.

Hush, chided Mira. *I think he's very sweet.*

Pen stared at that ugly boot-face, and tried to see what she was seeing. The horrible thing was, he could.

"What do you want, in your heart of hearts, Mira? Anything I can command, I will lay at your feet."

Sadly, fondly, Mira smiled. "My freedom."

Chadro was silent for a good long time, taking this in. At length, he gave an infinitesimal nod. "I'm a man of my word. Shall I escort you to the border, then?"

"That would be very welcome."

Chadro offered his arm again, and they strolled slowly back toward the coach. "If your duke proves sand, would you know how to find me?"

"I would."

"You are young yet—what, twenty, twenty-three? You might change your mind in the future. The future is a long time."

You have no idea how long, thought Mira. *I had no idea*. She had reigned in Lodi over a century ago, after all. "Would you still want me at thirty? Forty?" She smiled dryly. "Two hundred?"

"Yes," said Chadro simply.

"Cruel to give you false hopes."

"Crueler to give me none."

"Not really."

This is excruciating, said Pen.

Aye. The darling men used to imagine they'd fallen in love with me all the time. Most of them were actually in love with their own cocks.

But not all?

She sighed, silently. *No, not all. I might have surrendered myself to one of them, but the tumor in my womb overtook me first. I wasn't half past forty when I died.* She brightened. *It's lovely to know I can still hook them in.*

Yes, Mira. Now please throw him back.

I am trying, she pouted. *He's charmingly persistent.*

"Two dukes, eh?" Chadro vented a reluctantly defeated huff.

"One must seize great opportunities when they come."

"It seems some opportunities come too late. Or too early." He stopped and turned her toward him. "For all we did night before last, I never got a kiss."

Pen barely managed to get an arm up between them, fingers spread on Chadro's chest, as Chadro encircled Mira and drew her to him, leaned up, and pressed his lips to hers. Pen did not interfere as Mira returned it with grace, but chastely, as far from the wickedly inventive Mira of the bedchamber as he could imagine. No wonder she'd made men's heads spin. He was just glad he'd chosen a minimal sort of padding, hard to discern in the folds of the blue-green dress. The watching soldiers whooped and whistled. Pen sensed wide eyes behind the masks in the coach window.

"Freedom can turn to ash as well," murmured Chadro.

"I know," said Mira.

"You are too young to be so wise."

"You are too old to be so foolish. But you are kind, which is a rarer treasure than gold. May the woman you finally bestow it upon be worthy of it." She slipped out of his hold, and Pen skipped toward the coach, terrified lest some incriminating under-padding come loose in the heat. With a strained smile, Chadro followed and handed Mira up the steps once more, giving her copper-tipped fingers a last squeeze of sincere farewell. He clicked the coach door closed.

Pen fell into the seat across from Nikys and Adelis, wheezing. Some low-voiced commands from outside, and the coach started up once more, this time with six armed outriders.

Adelis looked ready to surge across the gap and throttle him. "*What just happened?*"

"General Chadro has charitably undertaken to escort Sora Mira to the border, and see her safely across."

"What?" gasped Nikys. "How did you bring that off?" Adelis jerked around to look out the window, as if making sure they were still headed in the right direction.

"All Mira's work, I assure you."

Nikys stared at him, wary-eyed even through her sequined trim. "So where does Mira leave off and Penric begin, behind that pretty face of yours?"

Pen thought of how Sugane and Litikone had blended together, after all their years, and Vasia nearly as much, and shook his head. "Should I live long enough, who knows?" Still reeling, he flung his head back against the seat and waited for his heart to slow. That had been *worse* than sprinting. "If my demon doesn't slay me by sheer terror first. Although then it will be someone else's problem. Consoling thought."

Nikys tensed as if she wanted to recoil, but in the close confines of the coach, there was nowhere to retreat.

Penric closed his eyes, and thought, *I swear to my god, Desdemona, if I ever again have to disguise myself as a woman, I'm calling in Learned Aulia.*

Ungrateful, Penric! But he could sense Mira's amusement. At him, of course.

A murmur from Aulia: *I'm not sure it's such a compliment to me, either. Are you saying I'm dull?*

Penric imagined a mental figure of himself flailing his hands in apology and backing away, which made Des snicker.

Des went on, *If you wanted a dull life, Penric, you picked up the wrong demon from that roadside out of Greenwell.*

Ha. Which of us picked up which? And what were wrong or right demons, anyway? All demons started identically, as unformed blobs of chaos escaped into the world from the Bastard's hell, or repository of disorder, or whatever it was. Each grew more different from all the others with every rider it came to; the differences redoubled as its riders accumulated over time. Des's theological argument that the Temple should not blame the demons for the imprints their riders left upon them was ongoing, and...not to be solved on a coach road.

The vehicle rumbled onward. After a few minutes, Pen opened his eyes and gathered his wits enough to caution, "No word of this episode must ever pass anyone's lips."

Adelis snorted. "Embarrassed, Learned? It seems late to find your pride."

"*Not one word*," said Penric, irritated. "If it ever gets out to your enemies at the Imperial court how Chadro let you slip through his hands like this, they'll hang him in your place, Adelis. And he doesn't deserve it." He added, more cruelly, "Or maybe they'll put out his eyes with boiling vinegar."

That won a real flinch, and Adelis dropped his gaze, if not ashamed, at least deterred. Although after a while he muttered, "If we ever end up facing each other across a field of arms, I may well *wish* I'd let him hang."

The last five miles to the border passed in brooding silence.

Chadro's high-ranking oversight saw them past the guards on the Cedonian side with utmost courtesy, and no questions asked. The hired coach ferried them the few hundred yards down and across the stream marking the boundary of the two polities, and up the next slope to the post of the Orbas guards. There the postillion let them off, was duly rewarded with a suitable coin, and turned his horses around to go back.

The men of Orbas, having watched their impressive arrival at the opposite guard-post, gave them a closer inspection. No one broke character yet. The two masked servants trailed dutifully, overshadowed by their dazzling mistress, who gave the guards to understand, without naming names, that she was traveling under the protection of a very high lord of Orbas indeed, who was looking forward anxiously to her safe and untrammeled arrival.

The closest thing to an attack was after they cleared the soldiers, as they suffered the importunities of three rival coach owners competing for their business. Adelis, in the role of Mira's manservant, shouted and cuffed them to silence and chose the one who seemed to boast the healthiest and fastest team. It wasn't till they clambered into the new conveyance that Chadro, watching from the far side of the ravine, gave Mira one last wave. Charitably, she waved back and blew him a broad kiss before he turned his horse and rode away, spine disconsolately bowed.

They were a mile up the road from the border village, with no sign or sound of pursuit, when Adelis at last threw his countryman's hat and the carnival mask to the rocking floor of the coach and bent over with his scarred face buried in his hands. His shoulders shook, and Penric wasn't sure if he was weeping or getting ready to vomit. Or both.

Of the three who had shared this journey, Adelis had borne the most frightening burden, and Penric fancied the mask staring up blindly by their feet was not the only one he'd been wearing.

Nikys laid a consoling hand on her brother's arm and squeezed, perhaps knowing better than to speak. Prudently, Penric copied her muteness.

VII

FTER THE FIRST change of horses on the coast road, Learned Penric skinned out of Mira's togs and back into his own, an awkward process in the close confines of the coach. No...not really his own, Nikys supposed, just whatever plausible garb he'd obtained from some used-clothing merchant in Patos after escaping the bottle dungeon, and before presenting himself to Nikys in her villa's garden. That bright morning seemed a hundred years ago, from this vantage. Undyed tunic, trousers, a sleeveless green coat that had once fooled her eye, or at least her tired mind, into accepting him as a physician of the Mother's Order (unsworn); the clothes, the man, the deceits, and all of their little company seemed worse for wear after their long flight.

"When you get to the ducal palace, Adelis," Penric said, beginning to take down Mira's elegant hairstyle, "there are bound to be a lot of questions about your blinding. I would ask you… beg you…" He paused to remuster his words. "It will likely make it much simpler for you if your tale is that the man who administered the boiling vinegar did a poor job of it, and your eyesight recovered largely on its own. Your sister's good nursing did the rest."

Adelis studied him. "You don't desire the credit? The reputation?"

"Not for that, no."

"So what is your role in this play? This time." That Adelis had grown mortally tired of playacting was plain in his wearied tone.

"I don't suppose I need a speaking part at all. When we reach Vilnoc I plan to find the main temple, and report in at whatever house of the Bastard's Order they have there. Once I establish my identity I can find my own way back to Adria." He cast a guarded glance over at Nikys, thinking of who-knew-what. Combing out his hair with his hands, he began braiding it in a single short rope down his back. "Although it might be well for you to come in with me, and use the Order's house as a staging area for your foray upon the palace. Get a wash, a meal, maybe a loan of clothing. Send a messenger ahead announcing your arrival who will not be ignored or shuffled aside. Rather than taking your host by surprise. This not being an attack."

"I suppose," said Adelis slowly, "it would be better not to appear wholly as beggars at Duke Jurgo's gates."

Even though they were? But no. Adelis was a man with a treasure of military skill and experience to offer, as desirable as gold to any leader as beleaguered as Duke Jurgo of Orbas. Penric was right; her brother should do nothing to devalue himself, here at the start. And since she was his whole train, neither should she. Pensively, Nikys lifted the servant's tabard over her head, folding it aside. Adelis had already shed his.

Penric sacrificed the last contents of their leather water bottle to wet a dirty shirt and try to scrub off his rouge and kohl. The effort left him resembling a man who had lost a tavern brawl and then not slept for three days; impatiently, Nikys grabbed the shirt from him and cleaned his face herself. He merely murmured, "Thank you." She merely handed the shirt back rather than throwing it.

The port town of Vilnoc came into sight around the next bend and rise of the road, and Nikys peered out the left window, eager for any orientation in her upended world. She'd caught only brief flashes of the sea in the past few miles, but here the shoreline opened out before her. Vilnoc sat athwart the constantly silting mouth of the Oare river, navigable to larger boats for only a few miles inland before rising turbulently into this hillier country. The town had tracked the river downstream over the centuries, stretching itself to the present waterfront with its fortifications, one of Orbas's few good harbors along this difficult coastline. Which was part of why the duke made the town his summer capital, but really, to Nikys's Cedonian eye the place seemed hardly larger than Patos.

The livery lay outside the city walls, where they dismounted from the coach and paid off the postilion. An ostler gave directions to the local chapter of the Bastard's Order, sited hard by the main temple, which was visible from the inn yard as a looming shape on a height. For once, when they entered the city gates, they gave up their real names to the gate guards, though not their titles; Penric kin Jurald, Adelis Arisaydia, Nikys Arisaydia Khatai. Penric, Nikys reflected, had not been very careful picking an alias back in Sosie, if that was his real surname.

The local chapterhouse of the white god was readily found, a place for Temple administration rather than worship, occupying an old merchant's mansion on a side street just off the temple square. Penric parleyed them past the porter by sheer assertion, then left them uneasy in the vestibule as he talked his way up the resident hierarchy. He came back just before Adelis was about to bolt. He was accompanied by a gray-haired woman in the white robes of a full-braid divine, with a pendant around her neck that signified some authority, or at any rate the porter and the dedicat set to watch them stood up and braced at her entry in a respectful manner that Nikys did not associate with devotees of the Bastard. She addressed Adelis as *General*, Nikys as *Madame Khatai*, and Penric as *Learned Sir*. The latter made her minions blink, and the copper-haired vagabond grin at them.

Nikys was then taken up to the women's dormitory by a smiling young acolyte, very interested in her tale. Nikys kept her answers brief. But it was such a relief to be in the company of women once more, even if only for an hour or two. The hen party that promptly assembled to get her washed and dressed reminded her of the fuss Zihre had made for Mira, although the results were less spectacular and more respectable. Nikys thought she resembled a plump gray partridge, and wondered if she might have looked less dull had she been able to borrow Mira's dress. Minus the extension below the hem.

As she was being fed and fitted, she thought back over all that Penric had done for them, for no benefit to himself if Adelis did not choose Adria. Or unless Duke Jurgo did not choose Adelis? Was that the chance Penric was waiting for, why he continued to aid them? Their reception here was by no means assured.

She did not want to move to Adria. She hadn't wanted to abandon Cedonia, for that matter, though she could not regret a moment of her support for her brother. *Beggars can't be choosers* the old saw went. So if you wanted choice, you must not beg? There was something wrong with that notion, when Adelis himself would shortly be begging a place from the duke.

What she wanted—well, she couldn't have what she wanted, now could she? Which left her not with choices, but with second-choices. Or maybe mixed choices, things she desperately wanted inextricably mixed with things she wanted no parts of.

I want my life to not be one continuous emergency for a while. Gods. She was so tired her *eyes* were throbbing. But she could not relax yet. This palace presentation still loomed. She must get through it without stumbling, for Adelis's sake.

And if, contrary to all this pointless fretting, the duke granted Adelis his whole desire? Adelis would be off at once to look after his new army, leaving his sister to fend for herself in a strange country. Installed in some safe-appearing box first, no doubt, but still, alone among strangers. She'd returned to her widowed mother's house after she herself had been widowed, four years ago, but that wasn't an option this time, with her mother still in Cedonia. *Safe in Cedonia,* Nikys prayed. That his father's concubine had been as much a mother to Adelis as his own noble dam was not likely to occur to his enemies; only his closest friends were aware of it.

Safe in Cedonia was not so comfortable a thought as it had used to be, Nikys couldn't help reflecting, as a breathless dedicat popped into the dormitory and told her it was time to go down to the entry again, the duke's page had arrived, and Madame's brother the general was already waiting.

In the vestibule, she found Adelis dressed in clean, well-fitting tunic and trousers, dark and neat. Without ornament, more soldierly than aristocratic, but that seemed exactly what was wanted; Duke Jurgo must prefer to multiply subordinates, not rivals. Someone had trimmed his hair back to military standards. The owl-feather red scars framing the glaring garnet eyes might be a bit unnerving, she granted, to a gaze not grown used to them. In another lifetime, she might have dubbed the effect *demonic*, except she now had much more informed ideas of what a demon really was.

He gave her an approving nod. "We look as well as we can, I suppose."

She calibrated for Adelis-speech and smiled at the effusive praise, standing taller.

He stepped closer and lowered his voice. Watching her. "Your infatuation with the sorcerer is over now, I trust. After all his antics in Sosie."

Her smile faded, as she contemplated the tangled complexity of all she'd witnessed. The lunatic absurdities of pubic lice and amorous generals aside...*I saw him pull death from a woman's breast as if drawing down wool from a distaff. And then spin it out into the world, following him like a billowing shadow. He sees in the dark.* She shook her head. "I have no idea what to think of him by now."

He gave a little chin-duck, as if reassured. She had no such reassurance for herself.

Speak of the demon. A quick, scuffing step on the stair heralded Penric's arrival. Nikys found herself gaping, as taken aback as her first sight of him in the garden of the Patos villa.

He had somehow obtained Bastard's whites in the style of Adria; a close-fitting, long-sleeved linen tunic buttoned high to the neck, with an upstanding round collar, open from the waist down with panels that kicked around his knees. Slim linen trousers. Pale polished shoes. Most riveting, on his left shoulder, the triple loop with silver-tipped ends of a full-braid Temple divine, the usual white and cream colors twisted with a silver cord signifying a sorcerer. Or warning of one...

Unfairly, the official garb made him look even taller.

The copper lacquer was gone from his clean fingers. His hair was still henna'd, if a lighter shade, and drawn back in a tight knot at his nape. His blue eyes were alight, and Nikys realized that she was seeing him for the first time in his real persona, free of dissembling.

A movement drew Nikys's eye to another figure waiting in the vestibule, a nervous youth of perhaps twelve in the tabard and livery of Orbas. The duke's page, presumably. He stepped forward and touched a hand to his forehead in greeting and salute. "If you are all here, Learned Sir, General, Madame, I am charged to take you to Duke Jurgo's secretary, Master Stobrek, who will take you to the duke."

They followed the boy out to the streets of Vilnoc, where the sea-softened light was slanting toward evening. Adelis dropped back beside Penric to murmur, "I thought you were done here?"

"So did I, but I was told I was invited. Which, from a ruling duke, means commanded. I have some small reputation as a Temple scholar, and it seems the duke collects such men. Scholars, writers, theologians, artists, musicians. A cheaper way to ornament his court than masons, I suppose."

Nikys had seen the famous buildings and fabulous temples of Thasalon, some of which had come close to bankrupting an empire; Penric was right about that.

"For display like a menagerie?" Adelis said dryly.

Penric's lips twitched. "As the duke neither rides them nor eats them nor puts them to the plow, very like, I expect."

They walked some four or five blocks following the page, turning twice, before they came to a broader avenue that ran from the top of the town nearly to the harbor. The ducal seat here was neither castle nor palace, but a row of three older mansions run together. Echoes wafted from one scaffolded end: hammering and sawing, the clink of chisels, and men's cries. The page led them through the middle door, unimpeded by a flanking pair of guardsmen who granted him familiar nods. They did stare openly at Adelis's face—and covertly at Penric's shoulder.

Nikys had barely taken her bearings in the marble-lined vestibule when a delighted voice cried out: "Oh, it *is* him! Most excellent chance!"

"Master Stobrek, the duke's secretary," murmured the page helpfully, as the man strode towards

them, his arms out in greeting. His sweeping garments were a cut above those of the usual palace
functionary, and he wore a badge of office on a gold
chain around his neck.

Adelis took a breath and stood straighter, but
the man walked right past him and seized on Penric.
"Learned Penric of Martensbridge! It is such an
honor to have you in Vilnoc!"

Penric smiled in a slightly panicked fashion, but
allowed the fellow to capture and shake both his
hands. "Learned Penric of Adria, for the past year,"
he put in. "I exchanged archdivineships. We have
met, ah...?"

"At that extraordinary Temple conclave in
Carpagamo. Five years ago, now, so I don't wonder
you don't remember me—I was just a clerk in the
Archdivine of Orbas's train at the time, and your
talents were only beginning to be recognized. But I
certainly remember you! I am instructed to tell you,
on Duke Jurgo's behalf and my own, you are most
warmly welcomed at the duke's table tonight."

Stobrek turned around and added, as a palpable
afterthought, "And you too, General Arisaydia."

Adelis's return smile was rather fixed. Stuffed,
in fact. "Thank you, Master Stobrek." He rolled his

eye at Penric in new question; Penric just opened his hands and shrugged.

Nikys bit her lip. Really hard. Even though she was probably the only person present who could get away with laughing at Adelis. And even though her doubts about Penric still ran as deep as a well. She supposed she could now be sure Penric was Penric. *Among other beings. But I knew that already, didn't I?*

As an afterthought to the afterthought, Stobrek continued, "And you too, Madame Khatai."

She offered up her sweetest smile in return, and murmured, "Thank the duke for me too, then, Master Stobrek." She was fairly sure only Pen caught the acid edge; in any case, his lids lowered in what might have been acknowledgement.

A woman arrived— no, a lady, Nikys placed her by the fine details of her dress and discreet jewelry. Dark hair bound up, no gray but not young. Stobrek looked up and said, "Ah," in a gratified manner. "May I present Madame Dassia. First lady-in-waiting to Her Grace the duchess."

She nodded graciously to him, acknowledged the two men with only the barest gasp at Adelis's disfigurement, instantly stifled, and turned to Nikys. "The

Duchess of Orbas invites you to make her acquaintance, Madame Khatai. Please, come this way."

The woman led Nikys toward the marble staircase, heading up to whatever maze of courts and galleries this improvised palace had acquired.

Master Stobrek added, "And the duke awaits you, General, Learned Penric. By your leave, follow me." They trailed him through a ground-floor archway and out of her sight.

It was becoming apparent already that she and Adelis had reached a safe harbor. So, she no longer had to be afraid every hour, terrified in anticipation of whatever new threat it might bring. Wasn't that enough?

VIII

DUKE JURGO'S TABLE rivaled that of the duke of Adria's, though Penric had put his feet under the latter enough times to not be intimidated by ducal splendor. But it meant the meal was prolonged, and there were obligatory musicians, after, and so it was not until late that he finally had a chance to catch Nikys alone. He had to intercept her coming back from the ladies' retiring room—not going to, no, and he hadn't *needed* Des to tell him that, thank you. He gestured, well, herded her out onto a gallery overlooking a small courtyard opposite the one where the duke dined. It featured mainly builder's scaffolding, shadows, and, he hoped, a scrap of privacy.

They leaned on the gallery railing side-by-side, frowning into the gloom.

"So, Adelis has his post," Penric began. That, at least, had gone quickly. Jurgo's eldest daughter had lately married the head of the polity to Orbas's west, a man with the peculiar title of the High Oban; his far border was presently suffering Rusylli incursions. Jurgo had been anxious to obtain General Arisaydia's experience with that foe. An expedition in support of the new son-in-law was being readied to march.

"Yes, Adelis seems very...I suppose pleased is not quite the word, since he's not so war-mad as to be delighted by an invasion. Engaged, perhaps. Already. He's not a man built for idleness." Nikys turned and rested her elbow on the balustrade, watching Pen in the half-light leaking from the rooms behind them. "What about you? Has the duke offered you a stall in his menagerie yet?"

"Mm, there were hints. He can't conscript me, nor could I accept on my own word. He would have to get the archdivine of Orbas to extract me from the archdivine of Adria. Who, since he only just extracted me from the princess-archdivine of Martensbridge last year, at some expense, might not think he's yet had his money's worth of me." Penric rubbed his forehead. "I certainly did him no good on my first mission to Cedonia." He looked up. "I asked you this once before. Have you taken any thought for yourself? Because I trust Adelis has better sense than to drag you after him to a war camp."

"Happily, yes. Madame Dassia hints that a place might be found for me as a lady-in-waiting in the duke's household. Not to the duchess herself, but to one of her daughters."

"Oh." Penric was taken aback. "That sounds… quite honorable. Safe enough."

"Yes, Adelis was very gratified by the notion, too. Although since the daughter in question is seven, what it actually translates to is the work of a nursemaid or governess, except with a better grade of cast-offs. The servitor's tabard is invisible"—she sketched a rectangle over her torso—"but one wears it nonetheless. Still, it gives me a breathing space. It's a relief not to have to make any more hasty decisions."

A more alarming thought occurred to Penric then. "Don't ladies-in-waiting rather risk being preyed upon by lords-in-ambush?"

"If they're twenty, maybe. I'm thirty. I've been defending my virtue by myself perfectly well since

I was widowed." She made a hard-to-interpret grimace. "It wasn't as challenging as I'd thought it
would be."

"Oh." He gathered his courage, and his breath,
and turned to take Nikys's hand. "Nikys, is there
hope for me here, with you?"

Dishearteningly, she took it back. "You will have
to be more clear, if you expect me to understand
you. Hope for what?"

"I'm told it's bad strategy to open with one's
high bid, but I'm going to. Marriage?"

A long, unwelcome silence greeted this declaration. Nervously, he called up his dark-sight to try to
read her expression. Every familiar line and curve
and dip of that face remained lovely, but it didn't
bear a look of love. Nor was it a look of loathing,
which would at least be some strong emotion. It
was more the look of a woman confronted with a
monstrous pile of chores that she didn't have the
endurance to face right now.

Well, of course, Des put in, uninvited. In fact,
he'd specifically dis-invited her to this dialogue.

Dialogue: two sides. Not three. Nor fourteen, Des.

*Penric, the poor woman is exhausted. I swear, your
timing is as bad as Chadro's.*

There is no *alternate timing that would have worked for Chadro*, Pen objected.

He was only out by a century, murmured Mira. Pen chose to ignore that.

"Is it the demon?" Pen asked Nikys, bluntly. It had been so before. More than one woman, attracted at first by his looks and whatever glamour she imagined hung about a sorcerer, had decided upon closer acquaintance that he was a walking quagmire, and wallowed away like a panicked pony escaping a bog.

After a little silence, Nikys said, "Not...exactly." It sounded as if her own answer puzzled her. "I suppose I had begun to think of Desdemona as like what my father's first wife was to my mother. Arrived first, can't be dislodged, supposed to be a bitter rival, in truth her best ally. That may be wrong, here."

"No, it's not!" said Pen. Des purred in amusement, unhelpfully.

"But it's not just Desdemona inside your head, is it? There's Mira, whom I did not expect." By her expression, she might still be getting over Mira. Or not. "And then I realized...that's not all. Well, I suppose I've had glimpses of the two physicians. And Ruchia—you've implied more than once that she was a clever spy. How much of our twisting escape do we owe to her? That's just what I've seen. What haven't I seen yet? Is there not one first wife, but ten? And I can't even imagine what the lioness and the mare might be doing to you."

"Not that much," Pen protested. "They're very old and muted."

She declared, "It is plain madness to fall in love with a man who has more personalities than I have fingers." She wriggled hers, as if in demonstration.

Is. She said is. Not would be. Dared he hope Nikys was as much of a grammarian as he was?

Unlikely, murmured Des.

"Also, I don't want to go to Adria," added Nikys.

Pen, wrenched by this sideways jink, tried for a neutral-encouraging sort of noise. It was all very confusing, but if he could keep her talking…

She straightened up, tilting her head back against a supporting post, and sighed. "It's not that I have a special aversion to Adria, although I would dread not being able to speak the language. You have to understand. I spent half my life trailing after my father or my husband or my brother to assorted military camps or postings. There are *reasons* some military wives cling like limpets to their homes when they are finally allowed to stop. I feel like a plant that's constantly been uprooted and transplanted, and never allowed to grow, never allowed time to recover enough to flower or fruit. Ready to wilt in despair, denied its nature."

"Some people relish the road," Pen offered, feeling his way forward. "Youthful adventure and all that."

"I'm thirty," said Nikys, flatly. "The desire to escape a home where one will never be more than the child is not the same thing as volunteering to be dragged through every ditch in Cedonia. I'm too old for *either* of those to be attractive." Her eyes narrowed thoughtfully at him. "You, I suspect, are a bird. Even roads won't hold you."

"Only because of the way we first met. You've never seen me at home, with my books," Pen protested. "I'm really quite sessile by nature. The only bird-like thing about me is my quill, flapping away. There are weeks at a time when my greatest danger is a paper cut."

"And the other weeks?"

You just saw some was maybe not the best answer. "It varies, depending on what problems land in my superiors' laps, that they think they can tip into mine."

"Something I did not know at twenty," said Nikys slowly, "that I do know at thirty, is that when a woman marries a man, she marries his life. And it had better be the life she wants to lead. Your life seems very...unsettled, to me. Very..." She seemed at a loss for the next word. "Anyway, it's plain I'm safe for now. No longer in need of your escort, or protection. You have finished your task, Penric. Perhaps you can find another woman to rescue."

"You could be in need of my...something else," Pen suggested desperately. "My merry wit. My vermin-extermination skills. My kisses?" Hesitantly, he raised a finger to touch the side of her mouth; she dodged it. "A person can have many different kinds of needs, all as real as rescue."

She shook her head and backed a step. "I wish you fair flight. But I want to put roots in the ground."

"You are not a plant. And I am not a bird. We are both human beings."

Her lips quirked, helplessly. "Well...one of us is."

A pleasant voice from behind them said, "Ah, there you are, Madame Khatai. Your brother is looking for you."

Madame Dassia strolled forward, giving Penric the polite, repelling smile of good duennas everywhere. "We should say our farewells down-stairs, and then it will be time for me to show you to your new room. The household is a little disordered at present because of the repairs, but this is actually one of the more spacious of the duke's residences for us." She laced Nikys's arm through hers and drew her away.

"You see," said Nikys over her shoulder, "I shall be well looked-after here, Learned."

"So nice to see you again, Learned Penric." Madame Dassia's nod was a clear dismissal.

Penric gave them both a weak wave, and allowed himself to be dismissed. He made his correct and civil goodbyes downstairs, exited the palace-in-progress, and threaded the streets back toward the chapterhouse.

She didn't say no, Pen, Des observed into his despondent silence.

It felt like no to me. She certainly didn't say yes!

Two blighted proposals of marriage in one day for you, then. Poor Penric!

Pen definitely ignored that one.

The stars overhead were a bright wash in a vault still holding a faint sense of color, some purple or blue too deep to name. Orbas, it seemed, shared the beauty of its sky with Cedonia, even if reluctant to share anything else. Penric still loved this boundless exotic sky, in all its moods. Even though he could never, ever touch it. Grasp it. Bring it down into a bag and carry it home. There were so many splendid things here, it seemed, that he could not carry home.

He'd not taken time earlier to write the letter to Adria reporting himself alive. He'd wanted to include the final report of Adelis's meeting with the duke, he'd told himself. Or had he been hoping, even then, that some last talk with Nikys would show him what he wanted to do?

He had to scribble something yet tonight, so it could go out with the earliest Temple courier tomorrow. Or, he supposed, he could just leave in the morning, and speed back to deliver his bad news in person. Writing home asking for instructions when he could already guess them was really nothing but a time-delaying ploy. A piece of diplomatic subterfuge. Or, to put it plainly, wretched foot-dragging.

In the small but private chamber that had been allotted to him in the chapterhouse, he carefully removed his borrowed whites, lit a brace of candles at the little writing table, lined up paper and inkpot and quills, and sat. The room was hot and close.

The quill felt almost unfamiliar in his hand, after so many weeks without it.

He sat for a long time. Scribble or sail? For once, Des offered no opinion.

At length, Pen offered up a curse in the Bastard's name upon the heads of all hapless men who made fools of themselves for women, bent forward, dipped his quill, and began to write.